FINALLY MINE

ELENA AITKEN

Also by Elena Aitken

Finally Series

Finally Yours

Finally Mine

Finally Fell

Finally Forever

Finally Free

Ever After

Choosing Happily Ever After

Needing Happily Ever After

Wanting Happily Ever After

Fighting Happily Ever After

We Wish You A Happily Ever After

Keeping Happily Ever After

Finding Happily Ever After

Seeking Happily Ever After

Cherishing Happily Ever After

Ever After: Volume One (Books 1-4)

The McCormicks

Love in the Moment

Only for a Moment

One more Moment

In this Moment

From this Moment

Our Perfect Moment

The Springs Series

Summer of Change

Falling Into Forever

Second Glances

Winter's Burn

Midnight Springs

She's Making A List

Summit of Desire

Summit of Seduction

Summit of Passion

Fighting For Forever

The Springs Collection: Volume 1

The Springs Collection: Volume 2

The Springs Collection: Volume 3

The Springs Complete Collection - Books 1-10

Destination Paradise

Shelter by the Sea

Escape to the Sun

Hidden in the Sand

Stand Alone Stories

All We Never Knew

Drawing Free

Sugar Crash

The Castle Mountain Lodge Complete Collection

Bears of Grizzly Ridge

His to Protect

His to Seduce

His to Claim

Hers to Take

His to Defend

His to Tame

His to Seek

Hers for the Season

Bears of Grizzly Ridge: Books 1-4

Bears of Grizzly Ridge: Books 5-8

Halfway Series

Halfway to Nowhere

Halfway in Between

Halfway to Christmas

Chapter One

IT HAD BEEN A LONG DAY. Correction. It had been *three* long days settling my twins, Sadie and Lucas, into their dorms three hours away. Fortunately, they'd chosen the same college, so I didn't have to figure out how to clone myself to be in two places at once. As it was, handling the move-out on my own, when their father bailed on the last minute with some feeble excuse about being *busy* that weekend, had been almost as much as I could handle.

Almost.

After ten years of dealing with Barrett's last-minute excuses, forgotten birthdays, and generally one disappointment after another, it was nothing we weren't used to. Sadly, I think the kids had come to expect it from him.

Not that it mattered. I'd handled it. Just the way I handled everything. I'd rented a truck and together we'd loaded up what felt like an unreasonable number of boxes and set off down the highway to their future.

After three days of climbing stairs and hauling boxes, every muscle in my forty-one-year-old body screamed for a hot bath and a glass of wine.

I gazed longingly at my tub, and the layer of dust in it. How long had it been since I'd actually sank into steamy bubbles? Had I *ever*?

Not for at least ten years.

There just wasn't time. Ever.

With a deep sigh, I peeled out of my worn jeans and T-shirt and hopped under the spray of the shower for a quick rinse before pulling a clean uniform out of the closet.

There was no other item in my wardrobe I wore more than the light-pink, thin cotton dress that was the uniform at Rosie's. As the owner of the little retro-style eatery on the edge of town, I probably could have chosen to wear whatever I wanted. But the customers didn't know that the chubby, middle-aged woman with her permanent ponytail that was starting to show a few lines of gray was anything more than the lady who poured their coffee and served them plates of burgers and fries. And they wouldn't care.

It was all about images. And the truck drivers, drunk college kids, and random travelers who frequented my diner wanted the experience of an *authentic* diner. So, day after day, and night after night, I stuffed my body into the dress.

I had to suck in a little bit to do up the dress. Eating nothing but takeout for the last few days probably hadn't done my already ample bosom any favors. The top button strained over my breasts. Having the twins when I was only twenty-three had changed my body in all kinds of ways I never would have imagined. Besides the stretch marks and thirty pounds I couldn't seem to shed, the most notable of those changes were the very large tits that made fitting into anything with actual buttons almost impossible. And that included my uniform.

I tried not to think about how quiet my house was as I flipped off the lights and grabbed my purse. At the last minute, I picked up the paperback on my bedside table where it had sat, largely unread for the last few years. Maybe I'd have enough time to read now with the kids out of the house. I pushed away the aching loneliness that would only grow stronger and more insistent now that Sadie and Lucas were gone.

With a sigh, I looked at the book again and fanned the pages through my fingers. At the very least, maybe I could skip ahead to the sex scenes.

Reading about it was better than nothing.

But I knew I wouldn't read any of it, just as I knew that despite my best friends' urging me to, I wouldn't be having any sex. That would require me to put myself out there. And even with the kids gone now...there was no time.

And even if there was, I would hardly consider myself attractive to any of the eligible men in town—if there were any. I'd done nothing but work and raise my kids for as long as I could remember. The concept of having my hair done had fallen away years ago, leaving me with long, thick, almost unruly hair in desperate need of a date with scissors. I was softer and thicker, with much rounder curves than I would like and my makeup routine consisted of mascara and lip gloss—if I remembered.

I didn't consider myself *unattractive*, but compared to most of the women in Aspen Valley...well, there was no comparison.

Twenty minutes later, I rushed—late—through the door of Rosie's after dropping the rental truck off and taking the bus to the diner. I'd given the twins my car to share while they were at college, and selfishly, so they could come home for visits. But it meant I'd be taking public transit until I could find a minute and a few spare dollars to buy a new one.

"Doris, I'm so sorry that I'm late." I stashed my things behind the counter before straightening up to meet the unim-pressed gaze of my longest employee.

It was almost impossible these days to find anyone willing

to work for minimum wage plus tips, let alone a decent employee who would show up to their shifts and not steal. I needed Doris, and she knew it. But she and Stan, my longtime cook, were almost like family. I had no idea what I would do without them.

"I really owe you."

"You do." Her lips were pursed as she assessed me, the way she usually did. "But it was for the kiddos." She managed a small smile. Despite her tough, almost sour exterior, I knew how much she loved Sadie and Lucas. She and Stan had practically helped me raise them when I bought Rosie's ten years ago.

Doris had worked for the original Rosie, almost from the time they'd opened the diner many years earlier. She had opinions on how every aspect of the business should be run, down to and including how my uniform fit on any given day.

I held up one finger in warning when I saw her eagle eyes take in the state of my uniform. I knew my dress was too tight. It seemed as if all my dresses were too tight lately. The last thing I needed was her to tell me.

"Thank you very much for taking care of things while I was gone, Doris." I gave her a genuine smile, because despite how prickly she could be, I did really like the woman.

My smile must have softened her a little. "How are the kiddos? Did you get them settled okay?"

I nodded and bit my lip with the surge of sudden and completely unexpected tears rushing to my eyes.

I didn't cry. *Ever.* Not when my husband left me. Not when my parents passed away shortly afterward in a car accident. Not when my kids moved out, leaving me alone.

Never.

Which was why the tear that slipped down my cheek took me completely off guard. I swiped it away and sniffed hard.

"Now, now." Doris patted my shoulder, her annoyance of a

moment ago forgotten. "It's okay, Jessie. This is what's supposed to happen. You raise them up right and you send them off. It's the natural order of things. Not keep them home forever, living in your basement like so many your age seem to prefer. Young people need room to spread their wings. You did good."

It was probably Doris's uncharacteristic sensitivity that caused the next tear to slip out. And then the next. It wasn't until she grunted in response and headed into the kitchen to commiserate with Stan at the griddle that I was able to pull it together.

I must be sleep deprived. It was the only explanation for my emotions.

For the next hour, the diner was mercifully slow. Only in the sense that it allowed me to make a fresh pot of coffee and pull myself together. I didn't want to think about what the slower days and even slower nights meant for my bottom line.

Because no matter how I ran the numbers, they weren't good. Business was going down more and more every month. But the bills weren't. I hadn't missed the new Closed for Business signs in the windows of the neighboring shops. Every day, there were more of them popping up as the land developer got to them. There were only a few of us holdouts left. It was only a matter of time before Trent Thomas got what he wanted.

I'd tried to fight it and, dammit, I still wasn't ready to let go. And that's exactly what I'd tell him at our upcoming meeting. Although with every day that went by with fewer and fewer customers, I couldn't help but wonder what exactly it was that I was fighting for.

The bells over the door chimed, filling me with hope as the dinner rush, little as it might turn out to be, began.

The bike vibrated beneath my legs as I pushed it faster and faster along the mountain road. Getting on my bike was my only fucking release these days. The only way I could leave the office behind and forget for a little while.

And I needed to forget.

At least for a few hours.

As the CEO of MultiTech Software, I was used to the pressures that came with business, but with the details of the latest takeover weighing heavily over my head, the stress was reaching a boiling point. Which was exactly why I'd broken out my Harley motorcycle.

The minute I ditched my suit jacket and Rolex and slid into my jeans and beat-up leathers, it was as though I could breathe again.

Nothing cleared my head like a long ride.

Except a good hard fuck.

My cock throbbed painfully, reminding me again of just how long it had been since I'd had that kind of release.

Why had it been so long?

I growled a little and shook my head as I pushed the bike faster.

I knew exactly why. The last woman whose company I'd enjoyed had recognized me. I couldn't have that. The last thing I needed was another fucking gold digger.

The moment any woman found out I was Shane Grant and, like so many in Aspen Valley, had more money than I could ever possibly spend in one lifetime, they very quickly made it their personal mission to help me with that spending.

I hated women like that.

Who only ever saw dollar signs when they looked at me. I was so much more than a fucking ATM card.

Using me for sex was one thing. That was an honest and equitable trade. I used her; she used me—perfect. But as soon as money got involved, it never failed: that same woman, who had been all about getting down and dirty, suddenly was more interested in a diamond ring.

No thanks.

Been there. Done that. One ex-wife was enough, thank you very much.

The yellow line of the highway passed in a blur as I drove hard and fast until finally, I was ready for a break. The neon lights of Rosie's on the edge of town beckoned to me. I'd lived in Aspen Valley for almost five years, and not once had I been to the out-of-the-way diner until a few days before when I'd stumbled upon it on a ride. And why would I have? Aspen Valley was full of the rich and the richer, and more uptight, fancy restaurants to cater to the wealthy than any other town I'd ever seen.

But the diner had a good cup of coffee, a decent piece of pie, and most importantly, no one I knew.

Chapter Two

BY SOME SORT OF MIRACLE, I had steady customers most of the night, the last table of four trailing out right before eleven. Perfect timing. My girlfriends were due for our weekly catch-up and drinks in a few minutes.

Once a week, no matter what was going on in our lives, we made a point to meet—mostly at the diner because I was inevitably working—and catch up with each other. We'd known each other since we were thirteen and no one knew me better. True family wasn't given to you by birthright, as far as I was concerned. It was the family you chose. My friends.

I wiped down the table and put on one last pot of coffee before the door opened, the bells announcing the arrival of Abby and Sandy.

"Hey."

I raised my hand in greeting, a smile on my face. I needed them more than I realized this week.

"Our usual booth?"

"You know it." I nodded. "Anyone need anything?"

Abby laughed and held up a martini shaker. "I brought mine."

I shook my head and laughed. The diner wasn't licensed, which meant it was probably a risky business move to let my friends bring their own alcohol in, but we'd been doing it so long, I hardly remembered I wasn't supposed to.

"I have a fresh pot of coffee on for you, Sandy."

She smiled her appreciation. I knew she'd have a little Tupperware container of Baileys to add to it. She always drank the same thing. Darla, when she arrived, late as usual, would have a flask of whiskey and unless it was a special occasion, Brittany would stick to soda water. Only very occasionally did she add a shot of vodka.

As for me, I kept a bottle of white wine in the back cooler. Before joining them, I poured myself a glass and had just re-emerged from the back when the bells over the door jingled again. I almost didn't look up, thinking it was Britt or Darla, but something about the air felt charged with the new arrival. I slid my glass out of sight and turned in time to see the customer head for a booth on the other side of the restaurant. "I'll be right with you," I called.

He lifted a finger in acknowledgment.

"Sorry, ladies," I apologized a moment later as I delivered a fresh cup of coffee for Sandy and empty glasses for Abby's martini and Darla's whiskey when she got there. "I'll just be a minute."

"Don't worry about it," Sandy said. She was the sweetest of all of us. There really was no other way to describe her besides sweet. "Don't rush on our account."

"That's right," Abby agreed as Darla arrived. "I was just going to tell you about—"

"Your latest sexy escapade?" Darla wiggled her eyebrows.

Abby smiled coyly, and we all laughed. It hadn't been long since Abby and her first true love, Phillip, had reconnected over a very indecent proposal that we'd encouraged her to accept that turned out to not only be super hot, but also a chance for the two of them to finally be together. Ever since, we'd been regaled with many tales of their very active sex life.

And I, for one, was more and more envious of my friend.

"Okay," I said. "Tell one story. But no more. Not without me." They nodded their agreement and I laughed. "I'll be back soon."

I hustled to the counter, grabbed a pot of coffee and a fresh cup, and headed over to where my new customer sat. I moved on autopilot, laughing to myself about what type of crazy antics Abby was going to tell us about next. I couldn't help it; I loved hearing about the amazing sex my friend was having. I might as well live vicariously through Abby. Lord knew I hadn't seen any action since my divorce—okay, longer than that. Barrett and I hadn't been intimate in a very, very long time before we finally called it quits on our marriage.

I was distracted, still thinking about my sex life—or, more accurately, lack thereof—and just going through the motions as I poured the coffee and slid it in front of my new customer. At least, that must have been the reason I hadn't noticed how fucking sexy the man was. Because the minute I looked...

"How are you to—" I damn near spilled the hot coffee on him as I caught a glimpse of eyes so gray, I had to take a second look to be sure they weren't silver.

"Careful there, sweetheart." He steadied the cup with his strong hands over mine. The simple touch sent a spark through me.

I pulled back quickly and tucked my free hand into my apron. He was older than me, but not by much, just enough that his dark hair was streaked with the slightest bit of silver. He wore head-to-toe leather, like he'd just climbed off a motorcycle. I glanced out the picture window at the front of the restaurant and sure enough, parked under a light was a very shiny, very sexy bike.

I'd always had a bit of a fantasy about motorcycles.

The thought struck me sharply. I was *not* fantasizing about this man. *Was I?* Not after mere seconds of putting eyes on him.

I pulled myself back to the moment. "Sorry about that. I wasn't..."

I let the sentence drift away. *What was I supposed to say?* That I wasn't prepared for such a hot biker with thick biceps that my fingers were itching to squeeze, and those crazy piercing eyes, and the sexiest thick beard streaked with silver that matched his eyes to be sitting in my booth? I mean, I *could* say that. It was the truth.

"What can I get you?" I asked instead.

He smiled, but just a little, as if he knew what kind of effect he'd had on me and was enjoying every second of it. My body tingled under his attentions. How long had it been since I was flirted with? *Was* he flirting with me?

No. Not a man like this. Not with me.

"How about a little sugar?"

I stepped back. Flirting or not, that was way too forward. I shook my head, hard. There was *no* way I was going to give him any sugar. I don't care how sexy he was, or how long it had been, or how damp my panties were just from being in his presence. *There was no way I was going to—*

"Sugar?" He pointed to the table behind me and the sugar shaker.

Oh. Right.

I turned to grab it, taking the opportunity to exhale. I placed the sugar in front of him with a little more force than necessary.

"You didn't think I meant something else, did you?" He lifted his eyebrow, and I knew my face burned red. I could feel the flush all the way down my chest.

Behind me, I heard the bells over the door jingle, followed by Brittany and Darla's voices, but the sexy biker's gaze didn't leave me. I took a breath and regrouped. "What would you like?"

"Now look who's being forward." He wiggled his eyebrows this time, but his eyes still didn't leave mine. They held me. Almost hypnotizing me. It was ridiculous, but I couldn't look away. And I wasn't sure I wanted to.

"I'm not...I wasn't..."

"Why don't we wait until we know each other a little better, sweetheart."

My face blazed even hotter, and I shifted where I stood because something about this stranger made me feel things I hadn't felt in a very long time.

His eyes traveled down my body.

Was it my imagination or did his pupils darken when he got to my chest?

Once more his gaze moved up and locked on mine. "It's nice to meet you, Jessie." He stuck out his hand, and I had to put the coffeepot down to take it. His grip was strong, and instantly, images of what his hands would feel like pressed up on other parts of my body flashed through my head.

"How did you know my..." I pulled my hand away as if I'd been bit. *This was too much.*

He chuckled and pointed to my chest, where my name tag was pinned.

I glanced at it briefly, as if double-checking to make sure it was still there, and all I could see was my breasts, straining and —*oh my God*—heaving, against the cheap fabric of my pink uniform dress. "Oh."

"Just the coffee for me, Jessie."

I nodded, but my face flared hot again when he added, "For now."

Just like every other night for the last few nights I'd gone riding, I'd only been looking for a cup of coffee.

Not a hard-on so intense I thought it might cause personal injury if I didn't stop looking at the curvy waitress in the pale-pink dress stretched tight across her tits in all the right ways.

Damn.

I knew I was in trouble the moment I walked in and saw her, and her heavy breasts popping from the top of her uniform as she leaned over the counter.

The last fucking thing I needed was a sexy piece of ass distracting me.

Or maybe that was the very thing I *did* need.

She was the exact opposite of the women I usually dated— or more specifically, screwed. And it had been a long time since I'd indulged in a little distraction of that nature. And Lord knew I was well overdue.

But this woman…

I lifted my mug and took a sip of the strong, coffee before I poured another dose of sugar in.

My eyes drifted back to the counter where she busied herself for a moment with something under the counter—*was that a glass of wine?*—before joining a group of women crowded mostly out of sight in the back corner booth.

I sipped slowly as I watched her.

She was older than the young, giggling, almost absurd girls I usually hooked up with. Jessie was a woman. She looked like a hard worker. A little tired, but not worn out. Almost determined. As if life was a challenge she was determined to conquer.

Why hadn't I seen her before?

I chuckled into my mug. I'd only been visiting the diner for exactly three days. It's not as if I knew anything about the place or the staff. And I knew nothing about this woman who was currently laughing with the group of women in the corner instead of checking on her customer. A quick glance around the place told me I was the only one. *Still, should she be sitting down on the job?* Not likely. And I was almost positive that was wine she'd taken with her.

Not that I'd rat her out. That wasn't my style.

But it *was* my style to press her up against the—

No. She wasn't my type. And Jessie didn't seem like the type of woman who'd bend so easily. She'd be a challenge.

Maybe that's exactly what I needed?

There was nothing like the thrill of the chase, followed by the conquest, that released the pressure quite the same way.

Hands on those full hips while I bent her over and relieved that building pressure. *Oh yes, I could picture exactly how—*

"Can I get you anything else?"

I'd been so busy imagining what it would be like to have her that I hadn't noticed Jessie approach, coffeepot in hand.

"A piece of pie, maybe? It's delicious."

"I'm sure it is." I didn't bother telling her I'd enjoyed a piece of pie every other night.

"Stan makes it himself." She gestured behind her toward the kitchen, where the stereotypically bald, with a potbelly, cook stood over a grill. "It's peach."

I knew from experience exactly how good the pie was. But there was only one kind of sweet I wanted at the moment.

"Just some more coffee."

"It's not too strong, is it?" It was, but I didn't say anything as she topped up my cup. "I made it really strong tonight because my friend usually adds—"

She cut herself off before she could incriminate herself.

Too late.

"Does she add some cream liqueur?" I nodded toward the table of women, two of whom were doing a terrible job of pretending not to watch us.

Jessie's mouth opened in an O.

Before she could protest, I added, "I didn't know you served alcohol here."

"We don't."

"Is that right?" I smirked and bit my bottom lip a little as I assessed her. "And I suppose that wasn't a glass of wine you poured yourself behind the counter."

Again, her mouth fell open, but only for a minute before she clamped it shut again and pressed her lips in a line.

"I wonder how your boss would feel to hear that you're—"

Just like that, her face shifted, so she was now the one with the grin. "I *am* the boss." She jutted out a full hip and shot me a satisfied look.

Now *that* was an unexpected twist.

"Is that right?"

"Surprised?"

I was. But it explained a lot. And left a lot more questions at the same time.

"It's pretty quiet in here." I dodged the question.

Her face fell, the grin slipping away. She sighed. "It never used to be. But...it doesn't matter."

Her eyes betrayed her words. I could see exactly how much it mattered. She was worried about the business slowdown.

I shifted in my seat in an effort to release the pressure in my pants that had only grown worse the longer she stood there. "Maybe I'll have that piece of pie after all."

She laughed a little, a sweet sound. But she shook her head. "You don't need to buy pity pie. It's fine."

"It's not fine." I reached for my coffee cup to keep from reaching for her. "Besides, I know just how delicious it is." I gave myself away. "I've been in every night all week." No point in keeping it a secret. "I haven't seen you before."

More than anything, I wanted to keep her talking. Her attention on me.

She put the pot down on the table. "That's because I was delivering my twins to college."

Twins? College?

My eyes went to her left hand in search of a ring. It wasn't something I usually cared about.

Usually.

No ring.

Once more, I met her eyes. "That would explain the absence."

She stretched her arms behind her back in a way that thrust her tits forward. My gaze homed in on the button that looked as though it only just barely held the thin fabric over her chest closed. I willed the button to let go.

It held.

"My first absence in almost ten years." She rolled her shoulders. "Too bad it wasn't much of a vacation. Driving a truck and lugging boxes isn't my idea of a break."

So, she'd done it alone.

"Speaking of which," she continued, almost talking to herself. "I suppose I better start looking for a new car."

"Car?"

She blinked, as if she just realized she was speaking aloud.

"You said you needed to look for a new car," I prompted.

"Oh, that." She waved her hand in the air. "It's just that I rented a truck to move the kids out and I left them my car to share while they got settled. But it's just an old...well, it doesn't matter. But I was going to surprise them with it and get something...sorry. I'm rambling."

She was. I liked it. She was off-balance around me. I *really* liked that.

"Anyway." She took a breath and smiled brightly. "I guess there's no rest for the wicked."

I was grateful to be sitting down, because there was no way

I would've been able to hide how hard that comment made my dick. *Wicked. I bet.*

And I'd certainly like to find out for myself. Not only that, but I'd also like to give this curvy beauty exactly the kind of break she deserved.

She rolled her shoulders back once more and picked up the coffeepot. "I'll go get you that piece of pie." She paused and assessed me. "If you really want it, that is?"

I swallowed hard. "Oh, I want it."

Chapter Three

"HE'S TOTALLY FLIRTING WITH YOU."

I refused to meet Abby's eyes. She always saw what she wanted to see. There was no way that sexy biker guy was flirting with *me*, of all people. Especially after I started rambling on about the kids and moving and the car. I groaned a little, so embarrassed by my complete lack of control.

"He totally is," Darla agreed. "And he's cute."

"I don't know about cute." *Sexy in a dark and dangerous way? Yes! But cute? No way.*

"I didn't get a look at him when I came in." Britt tried to turn in her seat.

"Don't look," I hissed.

Too late. She was already straining to see the man, whose name I still didn't know. I took him his pie and was going to ask, but my tongue tripped over the words and instead, I just kind of hurried away. Besides, it's not like it mattered. He wasn't my type. Even if I *had* a type. Which I didn't. It was pretty hard to have a type when you hadn't dated in years and the only man you *had* dated was a total loser who you'd ended up marrying because you got knocked up.

"I can't see his face." Disappointed, Britt turned around and sat back in her seat. She sipped at her water.

"Take it from me," Abby said. "He's sexy."

To my surprise, Sandy nodded in agreement.

"You think he's sexy, too?" I asked her.

She swallowed her sip of coffee and Baileys and grinned. "Very. I mean, that beard...the leather..."

"Maybe this is Jessie's *go for it* moment?" Abby, who'd come up with the whole idea of *go for it*, almost yelled. She clapped her hand over her mouth in an effort to keep calm. It wasn't working.

Especially when Britt agreed. "Totally. I mean, a *biker?* Sounds like it could be exactly what you need."

There were a lot of things I needed. And although I wasn't convinced that a biker might not be one of them, my friends were missing one very important detail.

"There's no opportunity here, ladies." And that was the problem. Even if I was brave enough to take a risk and cast my inhibitions aside the way Abby had when she agreed to spend the weekend with Phillip, this wasn't the same. "I don't have any offer to accept."

"Go make one." Darla picked up her whiskey and grinned over the rim of her glass.

I almost choked on my wine. "You want *me* to make an offer? Is that how it works?"

"It can work however you want, right?"

Could it?

I had to admit, the idea of having any kind of sexy experience that involved the stranger with the dangerous eyes sent shots of heat directly to my core. But it's not as though I could go up and—

"I think he wants more coffee," Sandy said with a nod of her head.

"Oh, I think he wants more than that." Darla wiggled her

eyebrows.

I loved my friends; I really did. And I know they meant well with this whole *go for it* pact that we'd made, but they didn't understand what it was like for me. Not really.

Instead of trying to explain it, I shook my head and pushed out of the booth to fetch the coffeepot for the sexy biker.

Even if I wasn't going to actually act on it, I had to admit it was kind of fun to think about what could happen if I let myself take a chance.

"Can I get you anything else?"

I topped off his coffee and tried to keep my voice level as his eyes met mine with a hunger there was no way I was imagining.

Or maybe it was the way the light reflected from the fluorescents. Because no matter what the ladies said, there was no way he could be flirting with me.

The man didn't respond right away. Instead, he let his lips twitch up into a half smile as I worked to keep my breathing under control.

"If there's nothing else, I should get ready to close up."

I turned to head back to the counter, somehow feeling his gaze on my ass, and for the first time in recent memory, I wasn't self-conscious at the size of it.

"Close up?"

"It is almost midnight." I half turned and looked over my shoulder. "That's when we close. Although I don't really know why I bother to stay open so late anymore. It's not like there's usually any customers. Except you," I added quickly. "And I'm not trying to rush you. You're welcome to stay as long as you like but if I miss the last bus, it's a long walk—" I stopped myself from rambling again as I realized all at once that not only did I sound ridiculous, but now I was just being stupid, too. Telling a complete stranger that I'd be walking home in the middle of the night was downright dangerous.

I shut my mouth and was about to rush back to the counter to pull myself together, but his hand on my arm stopped me. My instinct was to pull away, but there was something about his touch. It wasn't menacing or threatening in any way.

Slowly, I turned around, but he didn't take his hand off me.

"You're not walking in this part of town at this time of night."

He held my eyes with his, challenging me to disagree.

"It's not safe, Jessie."

Chances were good it was perfectly safe. After all, it was Aspen Valley. Even the worst neighborhood was perfectly safe. But there didn't seem any point in arguing that particular fact.

"Never mind how reckless it is to tell a complete stranger about it."

Heat flooded directly between my legs at the way he chastised me, as if I were a little girl and not a grown-ass woman.

"I'm sure it will—"

"If you were mine, I'd never let you walk home."

His words froze me to the spot and simultaneously sent a burst of pleasure to my clit.

If I were his?

Before I could reply to that loaded statement, he said, "I'll drive you home." It wasn't a question. As if the matter were settled, he dropped my arm, leaving the bare skin hot from his touch.

I opened my mouth and shut it again, unsure of what to say, which was stupid. Of course I should say no. I should tell him my girlfriends would drive me home. I was a grown woman, and I was perfectly capable of getting myself home safely. More to the point, I did *not* need to be told what to do.

But I kind of liked it.

I felt the heat in my face as my skin flushed with the awareness that I did indeed like to be told what to do by this sexy stranger.

Her creamy skin flushed all the way down the V of her dress to the pinked skin on the swell of her breasts before disappearing beneath the thin fabric cotton.

"You should be careful about what you say," I said sternly. "And who you say it to. You never know who you're speaking to." I lifted my eyebrows and tilted my head in dismissal before I could say anything else.

I'd already said too much.

If you were mine.

Those words had slipped out far too easily. But I couldn't help it. Something about her was at once both strong and delicate. And I wanted to know more.

A lot more.

Clearly stunned, she blinked and walked back to the counter.

I'd meant what I said about driving her home, though.

I waited a few minutes and tried to talk myself out of what I was about to do. I had no business getting involved with this woman. Not only was she not my type, but she clearly had some complications in her own life that would be anything but straightforward. And straightforward was exactly what I needed.

Sex. A release.

Not involvement.

Still. There was something about her.

I watched as she cleaned up at the counter for a few minutes. She was obviously trying not to look at me. Her body was tense, but aware. I wasn't blind; I could see how I affected her. And more importantly, how much she was fighting it.

But why?

I sipped my coffee and finished my pie as she cleaned up before she almost reluctantly rejoined her friends at their table in the corner. I had to turn my attention to the cup of liquid in front of me to keep from smiling when the group of ladies were very clearly discussing me.

She had a choice to make, and as sure as I was about almost everything in my life, I had no idea what she would choose when it came to her ride home. She didn't seem like the kind of woman who'd accept an offer from a stranger late at night.

Still.

I felt it in my bones. She'd say yes.

She brought me another refill of coffee along with the bill before scurrying off again without another word. But she didn't have to say anything. I could see the way she looked at me. The way her breath caught in her throat when she felt my gaze on her.

I left a twenty that would more than cover my coffee, wrote my message on the back of the receipt, and went outside to wait.

"This is crazy." I stared at the table and picked at a chip in the Formica.

"Not crazy at all," Abby said. "Taking a chance and having a little fun turned out pretty well for me."

It had. No one could deny that. When Abby had decided to take billionaire Phillip Conrad up on his indecent proposal for spending the weekend with him, it had worked out *very* well. Like falling in love and having the sexy-hot relationship she'd deserved to have her entire life, well.

But that was the exception, surely.

Besides, my hot stranger was just that. A stranger. Abby had *known* Phillip before. It was different.

"It's just a ride home," Darla said. But the look in her eyes said she certainly hoped it was more than that.

I looked to Sandy. She'd be the voice of reason. But did I even want her to be?

No.

And just like that, I had my answer. I felt it deep in my soul. Something about the sexy stranger was doing all kinds of things to my insides. Things I hadn't felt in years. Things I wanted to feel again.

But I had to be the one to take the leap. She was right.

I closed my eyes and remembered the words I was supposed to say. The words we'd decided as a group would be the indication for us to encourage each other. I took a breath and swallowed hard.

"Should I *go for it?*"

"Absolutely," Britt said as she rejoined us from a quick trip to the bathroom. "I have a good feeling about him," she added as she grabbed her purse from the bench next to her. "He has an...honest face." She grinned slyly.

"I thought you didn't see him?"

"I checked him out on my way to the bathroom."

I looked at the rest of my friends. They were all grinning as they nodded. No one disagreed with Brittany.

"So, I guess this is it?" A thrill passed through me despite the fact that he'd only offered me a ride home. Not hot sex up against a wall. Still.

Abby squeezed my arm. "Text us when you get home so we—"

"Get all the hot details," Darla interrupted.

"I was going to say so we know everything is okay." Abby laughed. "But yes. We'll need all the details."

They all turned to leave, but still I didn't turn around to look at the sexy biker stranger whom I was about to be left alone with.

"Oh, and Jessie," Darla said before they left out the front door. "Have fun. You deserve it." She blew me a kiss and they were gone.

I took a moment to pull myself together before gathering up the glasses and turning around.

But, when I finally did turn around, my bearded stranger was gone. His booth empty. My stomach sank.

Sure, I was nervous about what his offer to drive me home might mean. But nerves or not, there was a whole lot more behind the flutters in my stomach. It was excitement.

But now that he was gone...

I shook my head and sighed as I set to my cleaning duties. For a moment, I contemplated calling one of the girls back to drive me home, but ultimately decided against it. The walk would do me some good. It would clear my head and maybe give me some clarity to what exactly I had been thinking.

Something was missing in my life, that much I knew. But would I find the answers in a sexy stranger?

"I guess you'll never know, Jess," I muttered to myself as I started to clear his table.

He'd left a twenty-dollar bill, which was way more than enough to cover his bill of less than five dollars. But that wasn't the only thing.

There was a note.

A folded piece of paper with "Jessie" scrawled in tall, neat letters.

My breath caught in my throat. It took me a moment, but finally I reached for the paper and carefully unfolded it.

I read it once.

Then again.

I'll give you a ride on two conditions:

. . .

1)Hold on tight.
  2)Let go.

It didn't make sense.

Did it?

What the fuck did that even mean? *Let go.*

But I knew exactly what it meant, and my panties were wet just thinking about it.

He hadn't left after all.

But he was a stranger and—sexy as fuck. And the way he looked at me as if he wanted to rip my dress off and—*no!*

I couldn't actually be considering it.

But I did need a ride home...

Plus...I'd made the pact with my friends to *go for it.*

I tucked the note and the twenty into my apron, deciding at least for the moment to think about it until I was done with my duties. Maybe a little time, even a few minutes, would give me some clarity or make me see reason. After all, hadn't he *just* told me how stupid I was to tell him I'd be walking? Wouldn't it be even stupider to get on the back of a motorcycle with him?

Dammit, my panties had only gotten wetter remembering the way he'd chastised me. Not as if I were in trouble, but more like I was...naughty.

Getting on a bike with a biker dude could be the stupidest thing I could do. *Or* it could be anything but stupid.

I spent the next few minutes wiping tables, stacking glasses, and cashing out the till. Finally, I couldn't delay any longer. I grabbed my tips from my apron, took the note, and tucked it into my purse, before I hung up my apron. "I'm out of here, Stan." I peeked my head around the corner into the kitchen at my chef, who was still wiping up the counters and tucking food away. "You good?"

"Absolutely, darlin'. Are you sure you're going to be okay

getting home?" He crossed his arms and they rested on his belly. "You know I'd give you a ride if they hadn't taken my license, and my car."

I laughed. Even if Stan did still have his car or his license, there was no way I'd let him drive anywhere. His eyesight was so bad, he'd kill us both. He could only see what was right in front of him, despite the thick glasses he wore. It was a good thing he lived a few blocks away, or he wouldn't be able to find his way to work every day. Stan was just one more reason I had to make the diner work. He depended on me. The weight of the responsibility felt heavy on my shoulders, but I shrugged it off. I had other things to focus on. Big, sexy biker kind of things. "I'm good, Stan. I'll see you tomorrow. I'm going to go out the front. I'll lock up behind me."

He waved me away and it was time to make my decision. That is, if the sexy biker dude was even outside waiting for me. It seemed unlikely, but then again, so did the offer.

Damn. Even thinking about it made me horny. After all, it had been a very long time since I'd had sex. It was embarrassing to even think about how long it had been. But it was definitely somewhere around the ten-year mark. And the only sex I'd had before that…well, let's just say it was nothing to get too worked up about.

My friends were right. There was nothing to lose. Except a *really* long dry spell.

I pushed out the glass door before I could change my mind. I had a moment to collect myself as I locked the door behind me and then I turned to face the parking lot.

There he was. Leaning against the sexiest fucking motorcycle I'd ever seen. It sent a jolt through me. Intellectually, I knew he had a bike and that the ride he'd offered me was *on* a bike. But it was different seeing it. I'd never been on a motorcycle. Hell, I'd spent most of my children's childhood telling them how dangerous they were.

He grinned when he saw me—like he'd never doubted I'd accept his offer—and pushed up from the bike to walk toward me. Away from the protection of the booth in the diner, he was larger than I'd expected. Easily over six feet tall, with thick biceps and broad shoulders. I felt tiny compared to him.

I crossed the pavement, my knees shaking a little, my panties completely soaked because seriously, this man was smoking hot, a complete stranger, and I was about to get on a motorcycle with him in the middle of the night and that was exciting as hell. And the deal. It had seemed like such a good idea when we'd talked about it in *theory*. And sure, taking a risk and pushing outside her comfort zone had worked for Abby. But I wasn't Abby. I was a single mother of two and—it had been *way* too long since I'd been laid.

Plus, I'd agreed.

Take a chance, Jess.

What do you have to lose?

I probably could have come up with a whole list of things I could lose, but something deep inside me suddenly didn't care anymore.

"You got my note." Even in the dim light of the parking lot, his eyes pierced right through me.

I nodded.

"And you agree to the rules?"

"I don't really…" My voice shook as if I were a little girl, and he were the Big Bad Wolf. Hell, maybe he was. Still. *Pull it together, Jess.* I tried again. "I don't really understand," I admitted. "Hold on and—"

"Let go."

The intensity that he spoke with sent a shiver directly through me to my core.

"You strike me as a woman who needs to learn how to let go, Jessie."

Damn. Had he been talking to my friends?

But no, I knew they wouldn't interfere like that.

I nodded, because he wasn't wrong. And in that moment, any lingering doubts I had disappeared. It was time for me to see whether I was even capable of feeling the things that Abby and Darla talked about. To see whether it were even possible for me, after all these years, to feel sexy. To *be* sexy.

I agreed to his rules.

"Put this on." He handed me his helmet.

I did as I was told and the moment it was situated on my head, he grabbed me by the waist and pulled me close. I thought he was going to kiss me. Just like that. My whole body vibrated, suddenly desperate for the kiss.

Instead, he traced my jaw with one finger before he fastened the strap of the helmet under my chin. When he was done, he pressed his finger to my lips before he pulled it away. "Let's ride."

I hesitated, suddenly unsure. After all, I didn't even know this man's name. "Um...wait."

He turned around and stared at me. Hard.

"I don't even know your name," I blurted.

He smirked. "What was rule number two?"

"Let go." I repeated the rule. "But that doesn't mean I shouldn't know your name."

"Call me Dax."

Was that really his name?

Did it matter?

Let go.

"Okay." I paused. There was no way I was changing my mind. "Dax."

He grinned and his eyes flared even darker in the dim light. Without another word, he swung his strong, muscular thigh over the bike and waited for me to get on.

I'd never been on a bike before, but it couldn't be that hard. I moved closer and immediately realized my tight skirt was going to be a problem. It was short and snug over my ass. There'd be no way to get on the bike decently.

Dax must have sensed my hesitation. He turned slowly and looked over his shoulder. "Is there a problem?"

"No. I mean…" I shrugged and pointed to my skirt but he only grinned.

"Oh, I don't think that will be a problem." His eyes glinted in the low light of the parking lot before he turned around again.

There was no help for it. I grabbed the bottom of my skirt and tugged it indecently high before climbing up onto the seat.

The cold leather against my bare thighs was in a sharp, sexy contrast to the hot heat coming from my pussy. When Dax turned the key and the bike roared to life, the vibrations instantly hit the long-forgotten sensitive spot between my legs.

Oh shit. This was definitely turning out to be a good decision.

Dax reached his arm behind him and, with his gloved hand, stroked my bare thigh before giving it a squeeze. "Ready?"

I nodded.

"Rule one," he said. "Hold on."

The bike lurched forward, and instinctively I wrapped my arms around his waist and pressed my body into his back. The thrill of the bike and the danger of what I was doing, combined with the vibrations pulsing against my core, were so fucking exciting I almost didn't notice that he hadn't asked me where I lived.

Chapter Four

I KNEW she'd take me up on my offer.

And the minute she stepped out into the parking lot, my cock twitched in anticipation. But when she wrapped her arms around me...

Fuck.

I revved the engine, and she pressed those huge tits tight against my back.

I pushed the bike faster, racing down the dark highway. I hadn't asked her where she lived, but I knew exactly where I was going.

And it wasn't to her house.

Not yet.

I couldn't quite figure Jessie out. She didn't seem like the kind of woman who'd get on the back of a stranger's motor-cycle in the middle of the night. I'd met plenty of those women. Hell, I usually preferred them. The type who wanted to use me as much as I wanted to use them. A quick fuck, maybe two. Nothing more. Ever.

But Jessie...it was clear to me that she worked too hard and no doubt, she hadn't had any *fun*, let alone an orgasm, in far too long. Even so, she didn't strike me as a woman who was looking for a quick release. Of course…judging by the way she was wrapped tight around my back, pressing her tits into me, and no doubt, grinding her pussy against the leather seat, maybe I was wrong. She was not ready to go home, and I was definitely not ready to take her there.

I had other plans for Jessie. I pressed the accelerator harder and revved the engine, pushing the bike faster along the asphalt into the night.

It wasn't long before I reached the spot I'd been waiting for. The highway was fairly deserted, especially at that time of night, and I knew all the turnouts along the river, mostly because in the past, I'd used them to sit and think. But tonight, there would be very little of either, if I had my way.

I slowed the bike and eased it off the highway down the dirt road toward the river. As soon as I came to a stop, I turned the key off and used my booted foot to flip the kickstand down. Jessie pressed tighter against me and whispered in my ear.

"What are we doing?"

"Sweetheart," I answered. "I think you know exactly what we're doing." It wasn't my imagination that I felt her vibrate, so I let her press herself up against my back for a moment longer. Without turning around, I slipped one gloved hand behind me onto her bare thigh. I let it travel up higher, close enough to her pussy that I knew she could almost feel the touch of my leather glove. I squeezed, making her gasp before I released my grip and slid off my bike.

"Unless this isn't what you had in mind?" I took a step back, keeping my gaze locked on Jessie, her skirt rucked up around her waist, my helmet still on her head. *Fuck*. She looked sexy.

I waited for an answer. If I'd read it wrong, if she wanted me to take her home, I'd do it. I didn't let my eyes leave hers.

Finally, she swallowed hard and nodded. "No." Her voice

was soft, barely more than a whisper. "I'm not ready to go home."

My lips curled up in a reflexive smile. I hadn't read it wrong at all.

"Did you enjoy the ride?" I asked.

She nodded.

"What was that?" I took a step closer and pulled my gloves off before tossing them to the ground. I kept my voice low. "Did you enjoy yourself, Jessie?"

She made a small noise in answer.

I reached forward and undid the clasp under her chin, slid the strap through the buckle, and released her from the confines of the helmet.

Jessie pulled the helmet off her head and shook out her hair, so it fell over her luscious tits. Her nipples were deliciously hard from the cold night air, standing at attention, begging me to touch them. To pull them. To suck on them.

Not yet. I swallowed hard.

Instead, I threaded one hand through her hair until it cupped the back of her head. Jessie groaned as I used my grip to tilt her head up, her eyes closed and her lips parted. Her chest rose and fell in anticipation. As much as I enjoyed the sight of her wanting me, I needed to taste her.

With no further hesitation, I pressed my lips to hers and kissed her with an intensity that would leave no question about what it was I was after.

She moaned into my mouth and hungrily responded to my kiss.

I could lose myself in the taste of her, but I needed to stay in control. My free hand found her waist and squeezed a little.

I liked her curves. A lot. She was soft, her body plump and inviting. There was something to hold onto.

With one hand still firmly twined through her hair, holding

her sweet lips to mine, I let my other hand travel up her body until I found her breast.

She gasped into my mouth as my thumb stroked over her hard nipple. She pressed into me further, and I tweaked her nipple between my thumb and finger.

Jessie squealed in response and pulled away, but just a little. Her chest heaved so hard with her every breath I was sure those tiny buttons holding the thin fabric together would pop off at any moment.

"You still didn't answer my question," I said. "Did you like your ride?" I asked for the third time.

This time she nodded. "I did. But it's not over yet, is it?"

She licked her lips and my cock twitched.

"Not even close."

I stepped forward again, grabbed her chin in my hand, and kissed her. Hard.

I could taste the traces of white wine on her tongue, but there was something else, too. A sweetness I hadn't expected. Like honey.

Delicious.

When I could, I pulled myself away.

She was still sitting astride my bike, and I knew without looking her panties were soaked through. No doubt she was drenching my leather seat with her juices and *damn*, I wanted to stick my hard cock inside her and—

No.

All in due time.

Her willingness to play along surprised me. But I wasn't complaining. Not. At. All.

"Get off the bike." My words came out rougher than I meant as I tried to keep myself in check. She did as I requested. Jessie struck me as the type of woman who was used to making every single decision in her life. She was in charge of every detail, and she did a damn fine job of it, too. But she craved for someone to take control. At least in some small way, she wanted the opportunity to let go. She *needed* it.

I was happy to take on the task. If she'd have me.

And it looked as if she would.

She stood before me, her skirt still rucked up, her juicy thighs perfectly on display in the moonlight. I could smell her desire on the night air.

I slid one hand up the length of her thigh so that my fingers rested only millimeters from the cleft between her legs. "Is this your first time?"

I could feel her entire body resisting the urge to press into my fingers. She was barely holding herself back. It was sexy as hell.

"My first…I have child—oh." She stopped herself. "You mean, my first time with a…doing something like…"

I tried not to chuckle. "I meant, was this your first time on a bike?"

Her hand flew up to cover her face and her embarrassment. But there was nothing to be embarrassed of. It wasn't hard to figure out it was also her first time doing anything so risqué with a stranger. I liked that I would be her first. Gently, I took her hand away from her face and held it in my own, my other hand still on her thigh, squeezing a little as a reminder of exactly what was about to happen. If she wanted it.

"Jessie?" Her eyes met mine. "I'm going to ask you one more time if this is what you want." I paused. "If you want me to take you home, say the word and we'll go right now."

"And if I don't?"

I didn't bother trying to hide my grin. "And if you don't…" I moved my fingers close enough so she could feel the heat of them, but still not feel my touch.

She groaned a little.

"If you don't," I continued, "then I'm going to make you come so hard you won't remember your name."

Somehow, I managed to stay on my feet, but my mouth would not form the words to answer him. Who *was* this man and where had he come from? Never had a man spoken to me that way. And I liked it. A lot.

Let go.

And why not? It's not like it was going to be anything more than sex. That's all I wanted. All he wanted. Nothing serious.

I'd never let go before. Hell, I'd never even come close. I'd spent so much time keeping it all together for so long that now, on the side of the road with a complete stranger, I was considering…no. There was nothing to consider. I was going to let this sexy biker who kissed me as if his very life depended on it make me come.

And my whole body vibrated with expectation.

"So?"

He wanted an answer, but I didn't trust myself to speak. Not with his fingers so close to my clit that the only thing I could properly focus on was having his touch on me.

The combination of the adventure and the vibrations of the bike ride pressed up against Dax and his leather-clad, hard body had me so turned on that I thought I might scream if he didn't touch me soon.

I was greedy. I wanted more.

But I also wanted him.

Badly.

I'd shut off my brain the minute he'd turned off the bike and stood in front of me, demanding to know whether I liked the ride. Because he was right—I knew exactly what we were doing, and I didn't need any of that pesky common sense getting in the way.

Not tonight.

I'd never been so turned on by a man in my entire life. I

owed it to myself to let it happen; I was so long overdue to feel something. And to feel *good*.

"I'm waiting, Jessie." His fingers wiggled again, just barely brushing my pussy. I wanted his touch on me so bad it was almost painful.

I swallowed hard and closed my eyes. "Make me come, Dax."

A low growl rumbled from somewhere deep in his chest, but instead of finally feeling the touch of his fingers on me, he took a step back. I could feel the chill from the night air without his body so close.

I snapped my eyes open. "What—"

He held up a finger to silence me. "I want to see you." His voice was rough and demanding.

There was no way he meant for me to strip. It was a warm fall night, but still... I didn't strip. I could barely look at my own body in the mirror, complete with stretch marks and the extra pounds of too much diner food and not enough exercise. There was no way I could let this man see me. Even in the dim light of the night, there was no way.

I shook my head and tried to back away. If he wanted me naked, this would be over before it began. I just couldn't—

"Jessie." His hand clamped down on my thigh. Just enough to stop me from moving. "You're gorgeous." He looked me directly in the eyes when he said it and for a moment, I believed him. "I won't make you do anything you're uncomfortable with," he added. "I'll push you, if you let me. But all in good time."

His eyes were kind, and I believed him. Besides that, his hand was still so close to my pussy and the need for him to touch me hadn't let up. Not even a little bit.

As if he sensed what I was thinking, Dax chose that moment to finally, lightly, torturously so, brush one finger over my sensitive nub.

I shuddered and my knees buckled a little.

Without moving the hand on my thigh, he used his other hand to travel up the curves of my body to the tiny plastic buttons holding the top of my dress together. "Just this, then."

I nodded.

His fingers quickly pushed the little buttons easily through their holes until the cool air hit my breasts with a shock. I didn't think it was possible for my nipples to get any harder, but they ached and pulsed against the thin fabric of my old, faded cotton bra.

I was embarrassed by my ratty old undergarments, but with the way Dax was looking at me with nothing but hunger in his eyes, he didn't seem to notice.

"You have no idea how luscious your tits are, do you?"

It wasn't a question that needed an answer, which was good, because in the next moment, he once more moved his fingers lightly over my pussy, rendering me completely speechless.

And then his hand was gone from my leg as he pushed himself closer to me. His breath was hot on my mouth; his hand held my face in place so I couldn't close the gap and take the kiss I craved.

And then his other hand was on my breast, sliding over the thin, dingy cotton. I was thankful the light was dim so he couldn't see how old the bra was. Truthfully, lingerie wasn't very high on my priority list, and I just didn't have the budget for it. Although, at that moment, I could see how it might become important.

"Such beautiful tits deserve nicer things." In a flash, he tore the garment from my body. The material was so old, it gave away easily.

I gasped. Both from the shock of it and the cold air hitting my nipples. Dax's mouth was on mine, swallowing the gasp.

His tongue plunged into my mouth, taking the kiss he wanted, and I was eager to give.

His free hand covered my breast, and I tried to lean into the heat of his hand, but I was rewarded with a sharp pinch of my nipple. I gasped again and then groaned as he rolled the bud between his fingers.

Dax's mouth left mine. His beard was rough on my sensitive skin as he nipped, nibbled, and sucked his way down the length of my neck. I was breathless by the time he reached the swell of my breast. But I didn't have time to catch my breath before he pulled my aching nipple into his mouth and alternately sucked and bit down, clamping his teeth dangerously around the throbbing bud.

"Oh...I..."

His mouth lifted from my tender breast, replaced by his hand, which continued working my nipple further, driving me to complete distraction.

I was still wearing my panties, but I could feel my own juices start to drip down the inside of my thigh.

When Dax turned his attention to my other breast, my legs quaked with the effort of standing. His free hand clamped down over my ass cheek and squeezed hard, holding me in place as he lavished the same unrelenting attention on my other breast.

Finally, the desire that had been building from the moment I'd laid eyes on him in the diner threatened to boil over. My breath came in pants, and I tried to arch out of his touch, but he held me fast.

"I'm going to come," I whined.

I didn't want to come that way. Not that I didn't want to. Fuck, I did. But I wanted him inside me. Or his touch on me. Or... It had been so long since I'd felt anything like this—if ever—I didn't know *what* I wanted. My thoughts were jumbled. I couldn't form words to tell him what I wanted or didn't. I just knew if he kept doing what he was doing, I was going to come. Hard.

"That's the idea, Jessie. Come for me." The words were gruff. Then he bit down on the swell of my breast and sucked hard, while his hand tweaked the throbbing nipple on my other tit.

And that was it. I couldn't stop it. My knees buckled, but he held me up with his hand on my ass as I experienced an orgasm unlike any I'd ever had.

Chapter Five

I'D ONLY BEEN asleep for a few minutes. Or at least, that's how it felt when the ringing woke me up. I reached for my phone on the nightstand where I'd dropped it before finally falling into bed a few hours earlier. It took me a moment to gather my thoughts.

Had that really happened?

Had I really had a sexy rendezvous with a stranger who'd given me an orgasm on the side of the highway without hardly even touching me?

It didn't feel real. It couldn't have been real.

I ignored the ringing of my phone and slid my hand up and over my body to my breasts. *Yes.* It *had* happened. My tits were sensitive, my nipples had a delicious ache when I let my fingers brush over them, and when I flipped the sheet back to look at myself, I saw it. The faint outline of Dax's bite mark from when he'd made me come.

The memory sent tingles through my body, directly between my legs.

Never in a million years would I have expected to be standing outside, half naked in the dark, next to a motorcycle, letting a strange man, even a sexy one, do such wicked things to my breasts that I would climax. Of course, I had been looking for a lot more than some kissing and sucking when I got on the back of the bike. Truthfully, I was disappointed that we hadn't actually had sex. Especially after I got back on the bike, pressed against the vibrating leather, making me horny all over again by the time I got home, and he finally dropped me off. I'd thought about inviting him in, but it was late and…well, there was only so far out of my comfort zone that I could go in one night.

And I'd already gone so far out of it that I wasn't sure it existed anymore.

A laugh burst from my mouth. Instead of stifling it the way I would have in the past, I kicked my feet a little and squealed, giddy with the thrill of it all.

My phone rang—again. This time I flipped it over to see Abby's face on the screen, along with a list of missed calls from all of the girls. They were probably going crazy for details. Before I'd crawled into bed, I had managed to send a quick text letting them know I was home safe, but I'd left out all other details.

I pressed the button to accept the video call.

"Abby, I'm—"

"What the hell, Jessie? Do you know how worried I've been?"

I rubbed my eyes and looked at my friend. She genuinely looked concerned. "I told you I was home safe." It was lame, and we both knew it. If the roles were reversed, I would have been just as pissed as her. Maybe more.

She pressed her lips together, and I could see she was trying not to smile. "Hold on," Abby said. "I have the others on hold."

Of course she did.

I covered my mouth so she wouldn't see my smile. *Yet.*

A moment later, all of my friends' faces filled the screen in small bubbles. They all started talking at once, demanding information. I gave them a few minutes before I finally spoke. "So, you want details?"

I couldn't help but laugh then as they all instantly demanded that yes, they wanted *all* the details.

I didn't tell them *everything.* But enough that there were shrieks of excitement from all of them.

"Okay but wait," Darla said after a moment. "You didn't have sex?"

I shook my head.

Sandy tilted her head in question. "At all? Like—"

"I think she'd know if she had sex," Abby interrupted. "I mean, it's pretty simple."

"Yeah, yeah." Sandy rolled her eyes. "I meant…no…you know."

"No," Britt said. "We don't know."

Sandy sighed. "You're going to make me say it, aren't you?"

We all laughed. "Absolutely, we are," Darla said.

"Fine. I meant, no below-the-belt action," Sandy said forcefully. "You didn't have any oral sex, or penetration at all."

Abby burst out laughing. "Way to make it sound really clinical, Sandy."

My conservative friend shrugged, but they all waited for me to confirm, so I shook my head.

"Wait," Brittany said. "You didn't have sex? At all? But that doesn't make sense for Sh—that guy," she finished awkwardly.

"What?" I stared at Britt's face on the screen. "Doesn't make sense for who?"

"Sorry." She laughed and tossed her hair. "I just meant he seemed like the type of guy who would want to take it to the next level is all." She shook her head a little. "Sorry if I'm not making sense. I've been working nonstop."

That made sense. "I get it."

"Okay," Darla jumped in. "Back to the good stuff. He must know exactly what he's doing to make you climax with only some boob play."

He did know what he was doing.

"Either that, or I'm so hard up for a little action, that it didn't take much." I figured that was probably more likely. What I didn't say was that I was disappointed we hadn't had sex and I didn't know if we'd ever see each other again or if I'd ever have the chance.

It surprised me how badly I wanted that chance.

"So, are you happy now that you went for it?" Abby's question pulled me out of my thoughts.

I smiled and nodded. "I am. It was fun."

"It sounds fun," Sandy said almost wistfully.

"And that's exactly what this pact is all about," Abby continued. "It's fun to push yourself out of the boring ruts we've all found ourselves in. And who knows what it can lead to." Abby wiggled her ring finger, so the giant diamond glinted, and we all laughed.

But it was true. Who knew?

I was pretty sure for me, it wouldn't lead to much more than a fond memory of the time I let go, threw caution way out the window, and got on the back of a motorcycle in the middle of the night. But that was a whole lot better than nothing, and I'd take it.

A calendar reminder popped up on my phone, bringing me back to my reality. Which was far less about sexy strangers clad in black leather, and much more about trying to save my business from being scooped up by greedy land developers.

"I've got to go, ladies. I have a meeting with that land developer in an hour and I need to hop in the shower."

We said goodbye, with promises of talking soon and demands to know immediately if I saw Dax again.

I rushed through a shower before digging through my closet to find something acceptable to wear to the meeting. Not that it mattered what I was wearing. I wasn't a lawyer, and I couldn't afford one. We both knew that I didn't have many options and would more than likely be accepting the offer for the company to buy my building and my livelihood for a fraction of what it was actually worth. Still, I wasn't about to go out without a fight. Or at least, the appearance of a fight.

With my best bra lying in tatters in some roadside stop off the highway, I dug out another equally ratty bra. It was embarrassing that I didn't have anything nicer, but between keeping Rosie's open and putting two kids through college, nice bras were going to have to wait. But I really couldn't stand to lose any more, either. Even if it was in the heat of passion.

I'd gained weight since I'd last worn my back-up bra. It was a size too small, and I winced as I put it on. My breasts were tender from Dax's attentions, but in the best possible way. I wouldn't change it. In fact, I'd happily have it happen all over again. Just the way it had.

Well, maybe not *just* the way.

I'd fully expected him to fuck me. Hell, I *wanted* him to. Not that I wasn't satisfied. Because I was. I *so* was. But...

Maybe it was for the best. I'd only ever had sex with one man. And even then, it was definitely nothing too amazing. To say I had no idea what I was doing would be a vast understatement. I would have only embarrassed myself if things had gone any further. But...then again, Dax was a very take-control type of man. *I liked that.* And maybe he would have—

Jessie. Snap out of it. I forced myself to focus. Thinking about what could have been with Dax wasn't going to do me any good. Besides, I had a meeting to get through. An important one. The daydreaming would have to wait.

At least for a few more hours.

I hadn't intended on making Jessie come that way, but dammit, I couldn't help it. She was just so responsive and her tits…they were just too damn luscious not to worship them for a while. And fuck if she didn't respond to it, too. In ways that I never would have guessed. She was so sexy, so ready. Unlike any woman I'd ever been with. Jessie was different. In so many ways. And so far, in all the ways that mattered.

So far.

What was I even thinking? *So far.* That implied there would be more opportunities to see what type of woman Jessie was like. And there wouldn't.

I didn't date.

At all.

And Jessie would not be an exception. She couldn't be.

Still.

It had been exactly six hours and twenty-three minutes since I'd dropped her off at her little house on the other side of town. Six hours and twenty-three minutes that I hadn't been able to stop thinking of Jessie, her amazing tits, her curvy body, the fire in her eyes, her fierce independence, and most memorable, the little moan she made when she finally let go and climaxed for me. She was something special, that was sure.

I barely knew a thing about her. She had two college-aged children, she owned the diner, and worked herself to near exhaustion. That I knew. What I *thought* was that she was long overdue for a little fun, someone to take charge once in a while, and a whole lot more mind-blowing orgasms.

And I was rarely wrong.

The chime of an incoming email shook me from my thoughts and refocused me on the task at hand.

The merger.

My software company, MultiTech Software, was responsible for a series of programs that focused on the manufacturing industry and streamlining their processes. It wasn't as glamorous as Facebook or any of the other popular social media platforms, but it was lucrative enough in its own right. And it would continue to be lucrative as long as we remained *the* software of choice, which meant acquiring any and all startups that popped up in the marketplace.

Up until now, it hadn't been a big problem. There were a few who showed up with a new idea now and then that they thought they could make a go of. Most of them fizzled out on their own, and if they didn't, we would swallow them up. But this time it was different. Which was why this acquisition was so important. If SweetWater Systems continued in the market, they presented a real threat to my market share. And I wasn't about to let that happen. My lawyers had been working diligently on the details and we were getting close. But nothing was official yet, which was why my blood pressure was up, my nerves were shot, and I needed stress relief.

Jessie.

Maybe if I'd bent her over the seat of my bike and fucked her the way I'd planned instead of simply taking her home last night, I wouldn't be wound quite so tight. But it hadn't been right. Sure, she'd agreed to my rules, but that didn't mean she was ready for what I'd had planned.

Yet.

There it was again. The idea that I wasn't done with Jessie. Maybe another meeting wouldn't hurt. In fact, maybe it would be quite the opposite.

Just thinking about Jessie and the way her tits bounced when I tore that shitty old bra away so I could admire them properly made my cock thicken in my pants. I closed my eyes, and my mind filled with the glorious image. I shifted in my seat and leaned back a little in my chair.

"Knock knock."

I sat up so abruptly I almost smashed my knee against the desk. My eyes flew open to see my CFO leaning against the doorway, a knowing smile on her face.

"I'm not interrupting anything, am I?" It was clear that she knew she was, in fact, interrupting, but there was no way I was going to confirm it.

"Not at all, Brittany. I was just—what?" I tilted my head and narrowed my eyes. Brittany had worked for me for three years. She was smart, hardworking, and the best damn CFO I'd ever had. As far as I could tell, she didn't have much of a personal life outside of work, at least not one that she ever shared with anyone at the office. She was tall, blonde, and one of the most striking women I'd ever seen, and she was currently looking at me with a very suspicious smirk on her face. And I had a feeling I knew why.

"So that *was* you at the diner last night. Sorry. I wasn't in the mood to talk." I shook my head and ran a hand over my face. I'd been so focused on Jessie the night before, I wasn't really paying attention to her friends in the booth in the back corner, but I had seen a tall woman with the same striking blonde hair.

"Oh, I saw quite clearly what you were in the mood for." She didn't bother hiding her wide grin.

"You're friends with Jessie." It wasn't a question.

"She's one of my best friends." Brittany walked farther into my office and sat down across from me. "I was with Abigail Blakely as well. Phillip Conrad's fiancée. Maybe you haven't met her yet."

I shook my head. I hadn't met Abigail yet, but Phillip was a friend of mine and well known in the community and the snooty country club we were all part of. He was also one of the few club members I actually enjoyed spending time with. Learning that Jessie was somehow connected to my world was a completely unexpected turn of events.

A turn that might make things a little more complicated. Especially considering that with every minute that went by, I wanted more and more to break my self-appointed rule and see her again.

But she didn't know my name. Or who I was. And I wanted to keep it that way.

"Did you have a good ride last night?" Brittany had crossed one long, lean leg over the other and watched me as a cat might watch its prey.

I trusted her as a valued member of my team at MultiTech, but I had no doubt that if it ever came to it, she would defend her friend with a ferocity I didn't want to provoke.

Not that she'd need to.

I had no intention of hurting Jessie. Quite the opposite.

I leaned back in my chair. "I have a feeling you already know the answer."

She chuckled but didn't deny it. "Look, Shane. It's not my business who you go out with, or take for late-night bike rides," she added with a raised eyebrow. "But like I said, Jessie is one of my very best friends. So, *she* is my business."

I nodded, but Brittany wasn't done.

"She's not like the women you usually date."

I knew that quite clearly.

"And not only because she isn't just barely legal, with more tits than brains."

I couldn't help but smirk.

"Jessie is one of the hardest workers I've ever met, and she has a lot going on in her life right now. I agree with my friends that she could use a little more fun. Couldn't we all?" She added the last part more to herself, with a small shake of her head before focusing on me again. "But what she really can't afford is to have her heart broken, you know?"

Her heart?

Fuck.

"I appreciate your concern for your friend, Brittany. I really do. But you should know that I don't plan on…" I opened my mouth to tell her that I hadn't planned to see Jessie again, because after all, that was always my plan. One night. No ties. Nothing more. But I couldn't say it. I closed my mouth, swallowed hard, and finished the sentence, "Hurting anyone."

It was as close to the truth as I could get. And it was true. I didn't *plan* to hurt anyone.

But in that instant, my mind was made up. Screw my stupid rules. Jessie was different, and I *would* be seeing her again because I wasn't even close to being done with her yet. And if someone got hurt…well, hell. That was never the intention and I'd do my best to make sure it didn't happen.

"I hope you mean that, Shane."

"You know I do." I pushed back in my chair and tapped my pen against my knee. "But there is one thing."

She tilted her head in question.

"Don't tell her my name or who I am." It would be a whole lot easier to keep anyone from getting hurt if she didn't know who I really was. For everyone.

Brittany thought about it for a minute, but finally nodded. "Okay." She got up from her chair and crossed the room to the doorframe, where she paused and turned. "You should know," she said. "I was only okay with Jessie getting on that bike last night because it was you."

She was gone before I could ask her what that meant. It was clear that she knew of my reputation with women. *Why would she want that for her friend?*

Unless…

I could overthink it in a million ways, but there was no point.

"Mr. Grant." My assistant, Kenny, appeared in the doorway a moment later with his ever present clipboard in his hand. "Can we go over the schedule for the next week?"

I stared after the space Brittany had just disappeared into, but after a moment, I nodded. "Of course."

For the next twenty minutes, Kenny briefed me on the upcoming meetings I had scheduled, including all of the crucial ones with the lawyers regarding the merger. "I hope you're working in some downtime, Mr. Grant," Kenny said as he closed up his clipboard, the signal that he was done. "It's going to be a crazy few weeks and I know how—"

"I've got it under control." I pressed both hands against my desk. I appreciated his concern, which I knew came directly from experience. Kenny had been with me a long time. He knew how hard I could work and how hard I *would* work. He also knew what happened the last time I didn't take breaks or manage my stress. And I couldn't afford to end up in the hospital again with *heart strain* or worse, the doctor-ordered bedrest. I wasn't an old man yet. I didn't need rest.

But I did need a release to keep myself sane. And healthy.

I needed Jessie. All of her. Her body. Her mind. Everything about her. I needed it all.

Kenny gave me his look that meant he didn't quite believe me that I had it under control.

"I've been out riding my bike at night," I explained to him, although I was the boss and had no business explaining myself to anyone. "It helps."

My assistant nodded. "It does seem to help," he agreed. "And I will admit, you seem remarkably calm considering the chaos. Maybe you should go for another ride tonight?"

Now, that wasn't a bad idea at all.

"Maybe make them a regular thing until this merger is buttoned up. Whatever it takes, Mr. Grant."

Whatever it takes, indeed.

My lips curled up in a smile at just what those nightly rides might involve.

Yes. I definitely wasn't done with Jessie yet.

Kenny left me alone with a stack of reports to review, but my mind wasn't in it. I grabbed my wallet and my keys. There was something I needed to do first.

Chapter Six

"THANK you for meeting with me, Mrs. Bateman." A very tall, very handsome man in what had to be a very expensive custom-made suit stood from the table the moment I entered the restaurant, as if he'd been watching for me. He probably had. But even dressed in my nicest clothes, black dress pants that were probably three seasons out of style, and an equally dated silk blouse, it didn't take a genius to see that I didn't belong in the upscale restaurant where the meeting was to be held. The man held out his hand with a charming smile on his face that was no doubt meant to disarm his opponent.

And that's what I was, an opponent.

And maybe his smile would have had that effect on me a few days ago. But as good-looking as the sleek man in a suit was, he didn't even come close to the rough around the edges, raw sex appeal that Dax held.

I offered him a pinched smile and shook his hand as firmly as I could manage. "That's Ms. Bateman, actually."

"Of course." His grin didn't falter. "Trent Thomas. Nice to finally meet you. Shall we have a seat?" He gestured to the table behind him that had been set simply with two glasses and a pitcher of water.

I did my best to control my breathing as I slid into the seat across from him and pulled the letter his company had sent out of my purse. I'd made notes on the back of the envelope, listing all the reasons why I wouldn't accept his offer, but now that I was sitting there, it didn't seem very professional to put it on the table. Not that I was trying to appear professional, but at the very least I hoped I wouldn't come off as disorganized and taken off guard as I felt.

"I'm not sure what you were hoping to accomplish by asking for a meeting, Mr. Thomas." I started in immediately. After all, I didn't have much time to take the bus back to the other end of town, change into my uniform, and make it to Rosie's for the evening shift. I'd once more offered Doris over-time if she took the lunch shift as well as her usual breakfast hours. We weren't busy enough to require more than one wait-ress at any given time and the man directly responsible for that fact sat across from me. "I'm not selling my diner."

I folded my hand over the letter, which included the offer Mr. Thomas's company had made me for the business I'd dedi-cated the last ten years to. As if I could be bought. I set my lips in a hard line.

"Ms. Bateman, I can understand your reluctance."

"I don't think you can."

His smile was kind. In fact, everything about Trent Thomas seemed kind and genuine, but I was no fool. I knew it was an act to lure unsuspecting small-town businesspeople who just wanted to make an honest living into selling their life's work. People like me. So what if the diner wasn't my life's work? Hell, most days I didn't even like it. The constant pouring of coffee, wiping tables, serving pancakes or greasy plates of burgers and fries. Never mind the stupid uniform I wore while doing all of that. No. I didn't *love* it. Well, the dress…the memory of the way Dax had looked me up and down the night before, his gaze full of hunger for me and what was under the dress, flushed my face.

Okay. Maybe the dress wasn't so bad.

I shook my head in an effort to focus on the matter at hand. "Sorry." I wasn't sure what I was apologizing for.

"It's okay." Trent sat back in his chair. "I understand that this can be a stressful situation," he continued, his voice smooth and laced with concern.

It wasn't lost on me that he likely held dozens of meetings like this every day. He knew exactly what he was doing.

"But it doesn't have to be stressful, Jessie. May I call you by your first name?"

I nodded and then quickly shook my head. "Yes. I mean, yes, you can call me by my first name. But no, of course it has to be stressful, Mr. Thomas."

"Trent."

"Trent." I shook my head again. He was getting to me. I was rattled and confused, and we hadn't even talked about anything. I reached for the jug of water and poured myself a glass, which I drank slowly before I spoke again. "Trent," I tried again. "Of course, it has to be a stressful situation." My voice was controlled now. "You've come out of nowhere with an offer to buy my diner, which is my livelihood and without which I'll have no way to support my children through college." I didn't bother adding that if we didn't start getting more customers soon, I wouldn't have much luck paying tuition for either of those kids anyway. But that was a different problem. "That is the very definition of stressful, Trent."

"I can see how you would see it that way at first glance, Jessie. And I do apologize if it came out of the blue. That wasn't my intention."

I tilted my head in question.

He chuckled a little despite the fact that there was absolutely nothing funny about it.

I stared at him and waited.

"Look, Jessie. I know this is hard."

"You keep saying that."

"Do you really want to run a diner for the rest of your life? Surely you'd like to do something different now that your kids are gone?"

It was none of his business what I may or may not want to do with my life. "That's not why we're here, Trent."

"Isn't it?" He raised his eyebrows in question. "I'm not the enemy, Jessie. In fact, I might just be more like your fairy godmother."

The offer I had in the letter on the table in front of me was a lot of money, certainly. But it wasn't enough to make any of my dreams come true. Not even close. Before I could say so, he continued.

"The fact is your diner is in a desirable location that has been earmarked for development."

"You can't develop land that's already developed, Trent."

"I should have said *redevelopment*." Once again, his charming smile took over his features. "Even you have to admit that the whole area could use a face-lift and a little revitalization." He raised an eyebrow but didn't wait for an answer. "And most of the neighboring businesses agree with me. Ninety percent have already accepted offers, Jessie. You are one of the very few who hasn't seen what a great opportunity this is. Yet."

I opened my mouth but closed it again before speaking. He was right, and I hated it. The strip mall on the edge of town where the diner was located was in desperate need of a face-lift. It had been run-down ten years ago when I bought it, which was the only reason I was able to afford it. But now... shabby was being polite. Never mind that Aspen Valley had grown substantially in the last decade. Located just far enough from the city that was rich with oil money and more recently, big tech, Aspen Valley had become the premier bedroom community for those who were looking for a town that was big enough to have all the amenities they needed, but small enough that everyone who was *anyone* was known.

Those of us who'd grown up in Aspen Valley rolled our eyes at all the new residents, but no one could disagree that they injected a lot of wealth into the community. And with that wealth came development to support it.

The reality of the situation that I found myself in was starting to sink in. Whether I wanted it or not, was ready or not, progress was taking over, and I was going to lose my diner. There didn't seem to be any way around it.

Still.

I forced myself to meet Trent's eyes before looking down at the paper on the table. The number that was written there was a lot of money, but it wasn't enough. If I was going to sign away everything, I needed to be sure the kids' tuition was covered. They came first. I'd figure out myself and what I'd do later. When I looked back up at Trent, he had a small smile on his face.

He thought he'd won.

And just like that, I dug my heels in.

"I won't be signing anything today, Mr. Thomas," I said, abandoning the casual use of his first name. "In fact…" I pushed up from the table and tapped my finger on the letter, still folded next to my water glass. "I won't be signing anything at this price." I straightened my shoulders. "I know what I have, Mr. Thomas. And I know you need it." His smile flickered but to his credit, he held it in place. "You're going to have to do better than this." I pulled my purse up onto my shoulder and prepared to leave. "A lot better."

I hardly managed to walk out of the restaurant without tripping over my feet, I was shaking so badly. I'm not sure where the courage to stand up to Trent Thomas had come from, but whatever adrenaline was running through my body thankfully lasted long enough to carry me outside, where I used my phone to order a rideshare. It was an expense I probably couldn't afford, but it would cost me a whole lot more in the form of my pride if Trent Thomas saw me waiting at the bus stop after my little performance.

I allowed myself the luxury of closing my eyes during the ride across town to my house. There was no way to know whether Trent Thomas and his development company would make me a better offer or whether I'd just completely blown my chance to get out from under the crushing weight of the diner that was getting heavier and heavier every day. No doubt Trent had a whole office of lawyers ready to take my business out from under me without paying me a cent. If I had more money, or common sense, or both, I would have hired a lawyer of my own to protect myself. But there was no way I could afford that. And even if I was able to get some more money, I'd end up owing it all to the lawyer.

Taking the rideshare had saved me some time, a small detail I was grateful for. I could quickly change into my uniform and get to the diner before Doris's shift was over, which would give me some time to run the numbers from the last few days. I was pretty sure I knew what I was going to see, but still, it was best to know exactly where you stood when it came to things like this. Even if you weren't standing on very solid ground. Which I was not.

There was a white box, wrapped with a bright-pink ribbon, sitting on my porch. I bent to pick it up and instinctively looked around, as if whomever had put it there was watching nearby.

Of course, there was no one around. The tag on the box was addressed to me. That was it. Just: *Jessie.*

With a shrug, I tucked it under my arm and let myself into the house.

I tossed the package on the bed as I changed into a fresh uniform and twisted my thick, dark hair up into a clip on the back of my head. I was just about to leave when my eye caught the bright-pink ribbon on the box. I'd been so distracted by my thoughts I'd forgotten all about the mysterious package. But there was no way I was going to leave without seeing what was inside it. The fact that I'd ignored it as long as I had was some kind of miracle. I grabbed it and quickly pulled the pink ribbon away before I lifted the lid of the box.

Inside, was a note on top of tissue paper.

Replacements. Wear them to work.

Dax.

A shiver ran through me, and I tore the paper aside to reveal my gift. Wrapped in a single piece of tissue was the silkiest pair of panties I'd ever seen. If you could even call them that. There wasn't much to them besides some soft strings holding a triangle piece of black silk in the center. I rubbed my fingers along the fabric before I put the panties aside to pick up the matching bra. It was my size, but unlike any bra I'd ever worn.

I was already very busty. Some weight gain over the last few years had only enhanced the size of my chest. It's not that I didn't like my boobs. I did. But I usually downplayed them a little bit—or a lot—and I certainly never wore a padded push-up bra because...why? But the silky garment I held in my hand wasn't only far nicer and clearly more expensive than anything I'd ever worn before; it had *way* more padding. An indecent amount. There was no way I could wear that. My tits would be enormous.

I held the garments in my hand and contemplated putting them back in the box. I mean, it's not as if I could wear them under my uniform. They were black. And the thin pink fabric of my dress showed everything, which was why I usually stuck to white cotton.

I glanced quickly at the clock over the fridge.

Dammit. I was going to run out of time.

"Okay," I said out loud. I'd put them on. Because why not? I'd never received a gift of lingerie in my life. And knowing that this particular gift was from Dax, whom I never thought I'd hear from again…well, it made my body vibrate just thinking of it.

Let go.

Take a chance and let go. I'd done that last night and look how that had worked out. My stomach clenched in answer. Maybe the gift meant I'd see Dax again tonight. The idea of it made me happier than it should have.

I quickly shed my uniform and stripped out of my cotton underwear and bra. The effect of the lingerie was instantaneous. The second I shimmied into the little panties, I was turned on.

Holy shit. How had I never worn silk against my pussy before? The fabric slid over my skin and sent sizzling sensations right to my clit.

I put the bra on next, pulling my heavy breasts up and into place before turning to admire the result in the mirror.

Oh my God!

I was right; my breasts looked huge. Something about the padding of the bra had pushed them way up in a way I didn't think was physically possible. And the bra was cut really low in front, right across the swell of each breast, creating the most amazing cleavage effect. The bra was almost so low that I thought my nipples might pop out at any moment.

But damn, it was sexy.

I turned and admired the way the strings of the panties contrasted with the pale skin of my ass. I ran my hands over my breasts, down my hips and around my backside. The lift of the bra had the effect of enhancing the dip of my waist, giving my ample curves definition. It had been a long time since I'd looked at myself in the mirror this way. After all, there was no reason to. I'd gained more than a few pounds that I wished I hadn't and staring at myself wouldn't make me feel any different. But maybe I'd been wrong. Or maybe it was the lingerie. Or the fact that the gift had come from a very sexy leather-clad biker who had all but ordered me to wear it to work, presumably with the promise of more dirty things to come. Whatever it was, for the first time in recent memory, as I examined myself in the mirror, I liked what I saw.

A lot.

The reflection showed very clearly, a curvy, sensual woman who felt like a straight-up sex goddess in that moment.

A sex goddess who was going to be very late for my shift if I didn't hurry. Never mind arriving early to crunch numbers. I scrambled back into my uniform, struggling to do up the buttons over my chest. With my new massively enhanced breasts, the fabric was stretched to the very limits. The buttons strained as though they might pop open at any moment. But there were no alternatives. And I was right. If anyone bothered to look, it was easy to see the black of the bra through the thin pink fabric of my dress.

Oh well. Hopefully it would be a slow night without a lot of customers. Besides, usually my customers were all half asleep anyway. And they definitely weren't looking too closely at me.

All but one.

More than anything, I wanted a cup of strong coffee. As long as it was served to me by Jessie in the sinful lingerie I'd picked out just for her.

The ratty cotton bra and no doubt equally ratty panties, she'd been wearing the night before were an abomination, and they had no business being on the body of such a sexy woman. I didn't feel any regret for tearing them from her body. I'd do it again in an instant, given the chance. But as far as I was concerned, there better not be a chance to do it again. If I had anything to say about it, Jessie would only be wearing appropriate undergarments from now on.

My hands had memorized her size, and I'd made my purchases confidently, arranged for the delivery, and then almost immediately gotten on my bike and rode for hours in an effort to release some of the pent-up feelings that had built up since the night before.

It didn't work.

No matter how fast I went or how hard I pushed my bike, all I wanted was Jessie. I wanted my hands on her curves, my mouth on her sweet lips, my cock—*no.*

The very fact I wanted her so badly was the very reason I needed to stay away.

I was used to being in complete control.

And whatever I was feeling when it came to Jessie, it was far from control.

I passed the turnoff I really wanted to take—the one that would lead me back to Aspen Valley and the diner—and instead steered my bike farther down the highway, toward the city.

I left my bike and helmet with the valet of one of the more upscale hotels and made my way inside to the bar where my old college buddy, Trent Thomas, was waiting.

He took one look at me, clad in my beat-up leathers, and shook his head before lifting his drink to his lips. "You couldn't have dressed up a little?" He put his drink down, stood, and we embraced with a simple back-slapping man hug.

"What you see is what you get."

"Well, it's good to see you, old friend."

"Who are you calling old, old man?" I growled and dropped into the seat next to him. With a tap of my finger, the bartender poured me a whiskey and slid it in front of me. I nodded a thank-you and turned to Trent.

"It's been too long."

It had been years, in fact, since I'd seen my buddy, and we soon slipped into easy conversation. "Thanks for offering me the use of some office space," Trent said.

"You haven't taken me up on it yet." It had been almost a month ago that he'd called me and asked whether I had an empty office he could work out of while he brokered some deals. Of course, I didn't hesitate, but he hadn't taken me up on the offer yet.

"I will," he said. "I've been doing a lot of site visits and face-to-face meetings so far. Give me a few weeks, and I'll be desperate to hide in an office, away from everything."

"Do I even want to know what project you're working on now?" Trent and I didn't usually bore each other with details about our respective careers. I found his business of land acquisition about as exciting as he found software development.

Trent shrugged. "Same old, same old. But that's enough about work. Tell me, what's new? I ran into Phillip Conrad a few weeks ago. He seems to have found himself a hot new fiancée after all this time."

Abigail Blakely. We hadn't met yet, but I knew exactly who she was. And now I knew she was Jessie's good friend, too. Just another reason I should keep my distance from her.

Yet, just the memory of those delicious tits, and the little circle her lips made when she came undone for me, was all I needed to assure myself that staying away from her would be the very last thing I'd be doing. No matter what my common sense told me.

"What about you?" Trent asked. "Anyone special in your life?"

I almost choked on my whiskey.

Trent laughed and raised an eyebrow. "Is that a yes?"

I shook my head and wiped my lips. "You know me, Trent."

"I know you well enough to know that question rattled you."

I swallowed hard and thought about denying it. But what was the point? Besides, maybe an old friend who knew me well was exactly what I needed to remind me why I didn't get involved seriously with women. There was a reason I kept them at a distance. Sexual relief. A way to blow off steam. The occasional escort to a function. Nothing more than that.

"So, who is she?"

I ran my hand through my hair but didn't answer the question.

"Don't tell me you still think all women are nothing but gold diggers? You know that's bullshit."

"Do I?"

The last thing I needed was to get involved with someone who only wanted me for my billions. It happened far too often. I'd be dammed if it happened to me again.

Trent picked up his glass and took a long sip. "You should."

The thing was, there was no reason to believe it, and Trent knew that. Just like he also knew that I had plenty of reason to think the way I did. Her name was Courtney. She was tall and blonde, with tits that barely filled my palm. That should have been my first clue that she'd be nothing but trouble. I like my women busty. The bigger the better.

But something about Courtney had drawn me in. Later, I would find out that it was all part of the plan. She'd done her research. She knew who I was, and what made me tick. She knew exactly the buttons to push to have me eating out of her hand. And marrying her.

Without a prenuptial agreement.

She'd played me from the beginning, and I'd lost millions.

As well as my faith in love.

"I know she did a number on you, but not every woman is like Courtney. In fact, most aren't."

"And that's why I don't see a ring on your finger?" I raised my eyebrows and took a deep drink. I'd had almost enough of this conversation.

Trent laughed. "Got me. But I'm not fundamentally opposed to the idea," he said. "I just haven't met anyone who's quite up to the challenge."

That made me laugh, because I could absolutely believe it. I had no doubt that Trent would be a difficult man to be with.

"So, what's her name?" Trent said after a moment. "Because I know that look, man. And there's definitely a woman involved."

"She's not my type." *But she so was.* "But she's interesting."

"Interesting?"

I nodded. "I don't know anything about her." *Except how responsive she is to my touch. And the sound she makes when she comes.* "And it's not like that." I waved my hand, dismissing whatever it was Trent was thinking. "I'm just looking for a fuck. A stress relief."

Was I?

If that's all I'd been looking for, I would have taken it the night before. Jessie would have been more than happy to oblige. I knew that.

But something had stopped me.

Sure, I could have fucked her. But I didn't. *Why?*

I once more lifted the glass to my lips, this time swallowing the rest of the amber liquid. I was more than done with this conversation. It hadn't taken my mind off Jessie, who'd most certainly received her gift and, if I was right, had immediately put it on. My cock thickened at the thought of her tits pressed high, all but bursting out of that uniform dress. The scrap of silk between her legs rubbing her sensitive bud all night as she served coffee and pieces of pie to horny truck drivers who could only wish that they could have their hands on those curves.

But they couldn't.

They were *mine.*

I slammed the glass down on the counter harder than I intended. The thought of anyone else putting hands on Jessie fueled me.

"Gotta go." I tossed some bills on the bar. "Let me know when you need that office."

Trent laughed. "Tell me again how she's not your type," he muttered to himself, but I ignored him.

The diner closed in little over an hour. I needed to hurry.

And you wore it? To work? I grinned at the message from Sandy. The reply to my group text had come quickly. Sometimes I thought my friends were probably too attached to their phones. Either that or Abby was right, and we were all way too desperate for a little bit of fun. *But not me. Not anymore.* Thanks to my friends, and the push the night before, I was finally having that fun. And with any luck, I'd be having more of it later that night.

I quickly typed out my reply. *Of course I did. His note said to wear it to work.*

Do you think he'll be back tonight? It was Darla who asked.

Before I could reply, Abby's message came through. *Of course he will. Why else would he buy her sexy lingerie?*

Do you want him to come back? Brittany sent the question through, and I didn't even have to think about the answer.

More than I should. I laughed a little. I'd hardly thought about anything else. The night before had been fun, sure. But it had been *way* too long since I'd actually had sex, and I couldn't help but think that the next time I saw him, we would.

If I saw him again.

My gaze went again to the door of the diner. It hadn't opened in at least thirty minutes. It had been another slow night. And Dax still hadn't shown up.

He doesn't seem like the type. Brittany's message hit me in the gut.

But I shook it off. I might not know my mystery man well. But I knew him better than her.

Make sure you tell us all about it, Sandy said. *I have to run.*

The others all signed off the group chat and after I promised to fill them in on all the details, I tucked my phone away and set about wiping down the counters. Anything to keep me busy and keep my mind off the fact that Dax still hadn't arrived.

I'd been so sure he would come. After all, why give me the gift he didn't plan to see with his own eyes?

A shiver ran through me, contributing to the constant state of arousal I'd been in since putting the silk panties and bra set on. Something about the silk and the way it rubbed between my legs was delivering continual shots of pleasure directly from my clit through my whole body. I was sure that if Dax so much as looked at me, I might explode.

But he hadn't shown up.

It was almost closing time and I only had one customer. Hank was a regular who stopped in for exactly two cups of coffee and a Denver sandwich every Thursday. He was usually in and out in thirty minutes. Tonight, he'd been in his regular seat at the counter for almost two hours.

And he hadn't taken his eyes off me.

Or more accurately, my chest.

The same way most of my customers had stared at me all night. Even Stan in the kitchen had commented on my appearance when I'd finally arrived, a little later than I'd planned.

"Jessie, you look..." He lifted his spatula. "Did you do something different with your hair?"

I shrugged out of my jacket and hung it on my hook before grabbing an apron. When I turned around, I saw the old man's eyes, wide with surprise and an appreciation that should not have been there considering how long I'd known him.

"Yes," he said. "You've definitely done something different with your hair."

"She hasn't done a damn thing different with her hair in over ten years." Doris pushed her way through the swinging doors. "You're late. You said you'd be here——" Her mouth fell open when she looked at me, and for the first time since I'd met the woman, she was speechless.

I couldn't help but laugh at the effect my boobs had on my employees. But the laughter faded a short time later and turned into something different when I realized that almost every man I served all night spent a little extra time looking at my chest, and my tips had definitely been bigger. All because of my tits. Clearly, I'd underestimated the power of the female form. Of *my* form.

I had to admit. I liked the attention. Mostly.

"Hank."

He slid his coffee cup toward me, his eyes level with my cleavage.

I put the pot down and put a hand on my hip. "I've got to get ready to close up. Is there anything else I can get you?"

When he didn't answer right away, I bent down a little to meet his eye. "Hank? My eyes are up here."

"You look real good tonight, Jessie."

"Thank you. Can I get you anything else before I close up?"

He coughed a little to cover up his embarrassment of getting caught out. "I've never asked you this before, but... would you like to go out sometime?"

Surprise caught me off guard, and I took a step back. Hank was probably only a few years older than me. Not that I'd ever thought of him in that way. Or any way at all except for two cups of coffee and a Denver sandwich. I knew nothing about him. Except for maybe the new detail that he was obviously a boob guy.

"Hank," I started. "I'm flattered, but—"

"You don't have to answer right away. I know it's unexpected. I just got to thinking that maybe..."

He did seem like a nice guy. But I wasn't interested. Not even a little bit. Because the only man who held any interest for me at all was the one who'd given me the gift of the sexy silk that was currently between my legs.

I glanced at the still closed door.

Even if he hadn't shown up.

The sigh slipped from my mouth before I even realized it.

"Is that a—"

"Sorry, Hank." I needed to stop him before it got too far. I wasn't used to being asked out. It hadn't happened in so long. Much longer than I cared to think about, in fact. But I didn't want to hurt him. "I'm really not interested in dating right now."

He dropped his head for a moment before looking up with a grin. "How about just a—"

"I'm going to stop you right there." I held out a hand. "Before you say anything that will keep you from enjoying any more sandwiches in my diner."

He got the point. But he wasn't happy about it. With a few grunts of acceptance, he paid his bill and left shortly after. Leaving me alone and still no sign of Dax.

On any other night, I'd close up early. After all, what was the point in staying open for another half hour on the off chance that some bleary-eyed truck driver might need a cup of coffee they could just as easily get from the gas station nearby?

Of course, that gas station didn't exist anymore either. They'd closed their doors a few weeks earlier, having taken their own buyout deal.

Maybe it wasn't such a bad idea to consider the deal. They were going to get it eventually and if I really wanted to, I could relocate to a different part of town. Although the idea of starting over made my stomach turn and exhausted me.

My eyes glanced to the door and the dark parking lot outside. *Was that a flash of movement? Was it Dax?*

I waited and watched, my breath caught in my throat and my heart racing. But there was no further movement.

He wasn't coming.

Chapter Seven

FORCING myself not to go into Rosie's to see Jessie the night before was one of the hardest things I'd ever had to do. Generally, when it came to self-control, I didn't have a problem. I was the always firmly in control. But when it came to Jessie, she did something to me. She made me feel things I didn't want to feel. Which was why after my drink with Trent the night before, I'd driven directly to the diner and parked in the shadows of the dark parking lot. Close enough to see the object of my desire through the windows, but far enough away that she shouldn't be able to see me. Even if she was looking.

And she'd been looking.

My resolve almost broke when her one customer who'd been sitting at the bar and openly ogling her for far too long finally left. I wasn't an idiot; I could see the way he was watching Jessie. He was all but drooling at her magnificent tits. The bra I'd selected for her was perfect. The fact that she wore my gift filled me with pride. The way she carried herself, with a little more sway in her hips than the night before, no doubt because the scrap of silk between her legs was rubbing over her sensitive bud with every step, made my cock twitch with need.

She was gorgeous. The lingerie had only amplified her curves and enhanced what she already had. More than anything, I wanted to tear that thin cotton dress from her body and see the silky set under her clothes with my own eyes. I longed to put my hands over her curves and tear the new lingerie from her the same way I'd done with her old set. Because no matter how hot she looked in the black silk, she'd look so much better completely naked, her bosom heaving with the pleasure I would give her. Her breath coming fast, her mouth twisted with passion.

Yes.

That's what I wanted to see. I craved it.

Which was why I waited and watched unseen while she closed up the shop, waved goodnight to her cook, and got into her rideshare, alone. I still needed control, and a night of restraint would accomplish that.

But only one night.

One night was all I could handle. It had been torture waiting for the time to pass and it hadn't even just been about sex—although that was very much on my mind. I wanted to hear her voice again. Her laughter. The shy way she looked down when she was embarrassed or unsure.

It had been a long day waiting, and I forced myself to wait until after ten o'clock before finally pulling my bike into the diner parking lot and parking it under the flickering neon sign.

The bells over the door jingled, and Jessie turned immediately from the table she was serving to look right at me. As if she'd been waiting for me.

I paused and took my time, letting my eyes roam over her body, appreciating every bit of her. She was wearing the lingerie again. I could make out the string of the black panties on her hip, but to my disappointment, her apron hid the triangle of silk that would be covering her pussy. I moved my gaze up to her luscious tits, and my cock instantly swelled to life.

Fuck.

Seeing it from afar was completely different than appreciating the sight up close. The bra did exactly what I'd wanted. The black silk was clearly visible through the pale-pink fabric. Her tits were pushed high, the buttons of her dress strained, especially the top one, which was barely holding on. She was sexy as hell, and totally fuckable. Which was exactly what I planned to do later.

But the best part of the lingerie was what it was clearly doing for Jessie. She watched me watching her, oblivious of her customers, who were very obviously watching her—well, her tits—carefully. Her breath came in short pants, as if seeing me watching her, appraising her, was turning her on.

Maybe it was.

Purposefully, I turned away and went to the same table I'd sat at the night before to wait.

It didn't take long before Jessie stood next to me, her breasts so close to me, it took a lot of restraint to simply not reach up, pop the buttons of her dress and examine my purchase properly.

"What can I get you?"

I looked up and tilted my head. "No *hello*?"

She looked immediately and properly chastised. "Hello, Dax." She remedied it so quickly, it made my dick throb. "I wasn't sure if I'd see you again."

"And?"

Her smile was small, her lips curling up on the edge. "I'm happy to see you."

I liked her honesty. No games. I appreciated that more than she could know.

I returned her smile. "I'm very happy to see you, too."

Once more, I let my eyes roam over her curves. "I'm pleased to see you wearing your gift."

"Thank you for that." She stumbled over her words. "I mean, you didn't have to…it was unexpected and…well, I wore them last night the way your note said, but you weren't here and…" Her face bloomed with heat. She took a deep breath in an effort to compose herself and poured the coffee.

"I'm here now." I reached out and ran my hand over the curve of her ass before giving it a little squeeze. I knew no one else in the diner could see what I was doing because of the angle of the booth. I'd chosen my seat very purposefully. She gasped and a little coffee splashed from the pot to the table. But she didn't move away. In fact, she pressed back into me, just a little. "How's work tonight? Busy?"

"Busier than I expected." Her voice shook a little. "More than usual, in fact."

"Word must have gotten out."

Jessie tilted her head in question.

"About the sexy owner and her fantastic tits." I moved my hand down her backside to the hem of her skirt and slipped my fingers under her skirt so I could trace them up the back of her thigh to her bare ass cheeks. "Don't you agree?"

She sucked in a breath and shuddered under my touch, but still didn't move.

———

He was touching me.

Right there in the middle of the diner. Where anyone could see.

Holy shit, it was so hot.

I didn't think anyone could see me but knowing that they *might* turned me on.

"Why do you think it's busier than usual, Jessie?"

I shook my head. I didn't want to tell him that it was because of the way I looked in his gift. Or that I liked the way the lingerie made me feel. So much so that the moment I'd walked into my house the night before, I'd frantically rubbed the silky panties between my legs until I caused myself to orgasm where I stood in the front entry of my house. My coat and shoes still on.

I'd washed the garment specifically so I could wear them again tonight. Once again, the silk between my legs had me on edge the way it had the night before. Only now that Dax was here, his hand on my ass, that heat between my legs was rapidly turning into a full-fledged flame.

"Jessie?" he prompted, waiting for an answer to his question.

"It's probably nothing. Maybe there's—"

Dax pinched my ass cheek, hard and fast.

"OW!" I jumped and almost dropped the pot of coffee, but Dax's hand was gripping my ass cheek, holding me in place, and I was aware that there were other customers in the diner. Some of them shot a glance my way, but I smiled and waved them away.

"Jessie," Dax's voice was low, "you know as well as I do that it's busy in here tonight because all of those men can't keep their eyes off you. They're picturing your naked tits bouncing as they fuck you."

I sucked in a breath, grateful for the hold he had on me. I wasn't so sure my legs could support me at the moment.

"Look at them," Dax urged. "Look at the hungry way they're watching you."

I did as he instructed. My gaze slowly slid from the regular at the counter who'd already ordered three times more than he ever did, to the pair of young men only slightly older than my own children who'd been drinking Cokes and eating fries at the table in the corner for hours, to the older gentleman whose eyes hadn't met mine all night.

"Every single one of them wants you, Jessie."

I shivered at his words. Never had anyone spoken to me in such a way. It was incredibly hot.

"You look magnificent, Jessie."

Maybe I should have felt self-conscious, and in almost every other scenario, I would. But somehow with Dax, I didn't. I felt emboldened in a way I'd never experienced before.

"Your body deserves to be shown off," Dax said. "You look fantastic."

I *felt* incredible. And that in itself felt amazing. After my twins were born, the extra weight had never left me and while the rest of my friends looked incredible dressed in tight clothes when they went out to the club, I spent my days hiding in sweatpants and oversized sweaters, feeling worse and worse about myself. Over time, I'd just come to accept my body, but I couldn't say that I'd ever felt good about it. Until now. But it was more than the bra and panties. I'd be foolish to think it wasn't. It was the way *he* made me feel. Silk underthings worked magic. But not the same way the attentions of this man did.

"How does the lingerie feel?"

"So good." I smiled. "Thank you. It was very unexpected and unnecessary."

He laughed, a deep, rumbling sound. "Oh, it was necessary. I'm glad you like it."

"I feel...sexy."

Pleased by my answers, his hand, still on my bare ass, started to move in a soft, soothing circle over the sting of where he'd pinched. "Good," he said. "You should feel like a fucking sex goddess, Jessie, because that's what you are." He patted my ass and then his hand was gone. "You should probably get back to work. I didn't come here to distract you." His lips curled up into a sinfully sexy smile. "No. That's not true at all."

His eyes traveled down my front in a way that made my panties moisten in anticipation.

"I would very much like to drive you to distraction."

What was he suggesting?

"I'm not that kind of woman, Dax. I—"

"I know exactly what kind of woman you are, Jessie. You might surprise yourself."

Would I? It was one thing for him to touch my ass, but... where *would* I draw the line?

It was the craziest thing, but suddenly I didn't know. Two days ago, the very idea that I would be wearing sexy lingerie under my uniform would have been unthinkable. A man with his hand under my skirt? Straight-up scandalous. But now... the responsible, boring me had all but been replaced with a much more daring, adventurous, and *curious* version.

"What do you have in mind?"

Dax didn't answer right away, but instead his tongue slipped from his lips and he slowly, enticingly licked his bottom lip.

I tried to distract myself by pouring him a cup of coffee.

"You remember the rules?"

My eyes shot up to meet his. "Hold on."

"And?"

"Let go."

"That's right."

He nodded as if I'd passed a test I didn't know I was taking.

"I told you I'd give you a ride if you could follow the rules." His dark eyes flared with danger. "Do you want to go for another ride?"

Fuck. Did I ever. More than anything. The other night had

been amazing, but it hadn't been near enough. I wanted him inside me. I craved it. It's practically all I'd been able to—

"Jessie?"

I snapped out of my daydream just in time for the coffee I was still pouring to overflow the cup and spill all over the table.

"Oh shit." I moved quickly to grab a rag. Too quickly. My dress popped open; the strained button flew off and hit the tile floor somewhere beneath a nearby table. I grabbed the rag and started mopping up my spill.

"That's better." Dax looked directly down the front of my dress, which was now indecently open enough to see my cleavage in all of its pushed-up glory and the outline of the silky fabric. "I like what I see." He licked his lips again, which reminded me just what his mouth had done to my breasts.

My knees buckled a little with the memory.

Somehow, I finished cleaning up the mess, now aware that the tiny piece of silk between my legs was soaked through.

I moved to turn away and pull myself together in the bathroom when his arm shot out.

His hand wrapped around my wrist, holding me fast. "You didn't answer my question, sweetheart." His voice was low, thick with desire. "Did you want to go for another ride?"

I swallowed hard, because he already knew the answer. "Yes," I said without looking at him. "More than anything."

She captivated me, and for the next two hours, I watched her go about her work and tend to the customers she had who were, in fact, watching her as if they would bend her over a table the first chance they got. Not that they would ever get that chance. If I had anything to say about it, the only hands on that beautiful body would be mine. It was endearing to me that she had no idea how completely sexy she was, and how shy she was about showing off her fabulousness. It was a refreshing change from the women I usually dated, who all seemed to think they were God's gift to men.

Jessie was different. Really different.

When her dress had popped open, I could tell she wanted to fix it. Of course she did. I gently reminded her again of the rules: *let go.* I didn't know much about her, but it wasn't hard to see just how badly she needed to let herself go a little bit. Or maybe…a whole lot. So far, I'd been beyond impressed by her ability to switch off her need for control and do just that. And when she didn't immediately fix her dress, but instead wore it in a way she would never have let any of her employees, I was pleasantly surprised.

"Are you sure I can't get you anything else, Dax?" Every time she stopped by my table, her smile got a little bigger, a little flirtier.

To say I was enjoying the transformation as her confidence grew was a massive understatement. It was beyond a turn-on to watch her step into herself.

It had been an exercise in intense control to not fuck her the first night, and I'd never held off like that before. Especially when it came to keeping my distance. But it was exactly what I needed because I once more had control of myself and the situation. Besides, it never hurt to keep a woman wanting more. And judging by the dampness between her legs, where my fingers were currently doing a teasing dance with her clit, she definitely wanted more.

"I'm good with coffee refills, sweetheart. Keep them coming and maybe I'll make you come again."

She blushed hard, all the way down to her tits, which I could now see much better thanks to the blown button. It was the perfect view.

I was teasing, because I had no intention of sharing her glorious climaxes with anyone else, the least of whom were some random truck drivers fueling up with her thick coffee before hitting the highway again. I didn't need to give them any more jerk-off material than Jessie's tits already no doubt had.

But it didn't mean I didn't enjoy teasing her and pushing every one of her boundaries.

"Tell me…" I'd been asking questions about her every time she came to pour me more coffee, because despite myself, I wanted to know everything about her. "What made you decide to open a diner, of all things? Did you have an intense desire to make strong coffee?"

She laughed a little. "Not even a little. I just sort of fell into it. When my husband—my *ex*-husband—left, I needed a job I could do and still be around for my kids."

There were a million jobs that fit that description, but I didn't say so.

"I had a bit of money from an inheritance when my parents passed away."

"I'm sorry to hear about your parents."

She shrugged but I could see the sadness that clouded her eyes. "Barrett couldn't touch the money they left me."

Barrett. So that was the name of the complete moron who could walk away from a woman like Jessie.

"Buying the diner seemed like a good option," she continued. "And really the only one I had."

"But you don't love it." It wasn't a question.

She shrugged and moved to walk away, but my hand was still between her legs. She shot me a look, and I grinned. I wasn't done talking yet.

"No," she said after a moment. "I don't hate it. But it's just a job and now that the kids are gone…" She shrugged a little. "Well…maybe it's time I consider other things."

There was something she wasn't telling me, but I didn't

want to push. Not yet. She was already opening up more than I'd expected.

"What are you passionate about?"

Her laughter caught me off guard.

"What?"

"What am I passionate about?"

I waited.

"I used to enjoy painting. But what does that matter?"

It mattered a lot, but I couldn't tell her that. Just like I couldn't tell her that I had enough money to make all her dreams come true, if only she knew what they were.

Instead, I said, "It matters. It always matters."

Her face dipped into a strange look, but before she could say anything, I dragged a finger along the wet silk over her pussy, causing her entire body to tremble.

I shrugged casually. "Couldn't help myself."

She squirmed, but I didn't remove my hand, letting her know that I wasn't done with the conversation. The more I learned about Jessie, the more I wanted to know.

"What about you?" she asked, catching me off guard. "What do you do for a living? I've already told you so much about myself—tell me something about you, Dax."

It was only a matter of time before she asked me about myself, and I was ready with a generic answer, because there was no way I was going to tell her who I really was and ruin what I was starting to think could potentially be something real. "I'm in sales. It's not a big deal."

"Sales? What do you sell?" She tried to wiggle away from my now probing fingers, but I held her in place by cupping her sweet pussy in my hand. It was downright sinful what I was doing to her in the middle of her diner, and the very fact she was not only letting me, but enjoying it, spoke to exactly how much she was ready to let go.

"Nothing very well." I laughed and waved a hand up and down, in an effort to encompass my beat-up leathers. I'd slipped up by buying her expensive lingerie, but I'd hoped she had no idea what they actually cost. The same with my bike. If she'd known anything about motorcycles, she might know it was a custom build that cost more than her house. "It's a job," I continued. "But—"

"You're not passionate about it, either?"

"No," I answered, slowly and honestly. I'd never been passionate about software development. Sure, I'd enjoyed the challenges. But they weren't what got me out of bed in the morning. Of course, the only thing getting me out of bed right now was her. Not that I was going to tell her that. Just like I wasn't going to tell her who I really was. She couldn't know I had money. Not until I knew she wanted me for me.

Less than a week ago, that thought would have been completely unfathomable. But now...the idea of her wanting me and me wanting her...well, I liked it. A lot.

"Well, it's never too late, right?" She smiled sweetly at me. "Maybe we both need to do some searching for what we're passionate about?"

"Jessie, sweetheart." I worked hard to control my voice. "I have a feeling it won't be long before we've both found all the passion we need. Now, isn't it time to close up?" I gestured to the clock over the counter, threw down a twenty, and with one final wiggle of my fingers, pulled my hand out from under her skirt. "I'll wait outside."

It wasn't my imagination that I saw her entire body tremble with the promise in my words.

Chapter Eight

THIS TIME when I straddled his motorcycle and held on tight to Dax's leather-clad back, it was different. Not only had I been waiting all night—or, more accurately, two nights—to be with Dax again, but this time I knew him better. Or at least it felt as if I did. Even though I'd been working, it felt almost like a first date with him asking me so many questions about myself. And he was genuinely interested, too.

He was easy to talk to and despite the fact that I didn't know much about him, I was starting to feel myself actually falling for him. *Was that even possible? To fall for a man you barely knew?*

Of course it was—that's what had happened to Abby, wasn't it? Besides, just like she kept insisting, sometimes you just had to let yourself go a little and live in the moment. After all, taking that chance had sure worked out for her.

Maybe it might work for me, too. At the very least, I was going to have a little fun while I was seeing what could happen.

And I was going to have that fun soon.

The vibrations of the bike between my legs made me even hotter. *How had I gone my whole life and not known about the incredibly erotic effect of a motorcycle?* I wrapped my arms tighter and squeezed. In response, Dax accelerated, and we flew faster down the dark highway.

As soon as we parked along the river, in what I assumed was the same spot as the night before, Dax jumped off the bike and turned to face me, still sitting astride his bike.

He stroked his beard and assessed me for a moment. "Helmet," he finally said.

I reached up and unfastened the helmet before I handed it to him. Without being told, I reached up and took my hair down, letting it spill down over my shoulders.

He nodded appreciatively and then said, "Uniform."

I tilted my head in question. He'd wanted this the other night. For me to bare myself. But...I shook my head and moved to get off the bike.

"No." He stopped me. "Jessie."

"I've had children," I protested. "There are—"

"I know without a single doubt that your body is perfect."

Even in the dim light, I could see the silver flash of his eyes as he looked so deeply into mine and spoke with such confidence that I had no choice but to believe him.

"But..." I glanced around. "Anyone could come by."

His lips twitched up into a grin and his nostrils flared. "They could," he said simply. "And then they, too, will see just how sexy you are."

The idea of getting caught sent a thrill through me the same way his bold fingers in the diner had.

"Take off your uniform. Now," he added with a firmness that turned me on.

I hesitated another moment, but ultimately, I was going to do it. Rule number two: *let go.*

With a hard swallow, I did as he requested. I worked the buttons through the holes in front of my dress and pulled the garment from my shoulders. I handed it to him, but he tossed it aside and stepped back.

The night was chilly, but the leather seat of the bike was still warm between my legs from our ride, and I wasn't cold at all. Especially not with the way he looked at me. The moonlight reflected the desire in his eyes as he assessed me. I trembled in anticipation of what would happen, because something *was* going to happen. Of that much, I was sure.

And I certainly hoped tonight it involved his cock, because it was all I could think of.

"Damn, that's a delicious sight." Dax took a step back, admiring me openly. "Silk looks amazing on you."

Under his watchful gaze, I felt emboldened. I leaned back and put my hands behind me on the seat so I could press my breasts up into the moonlight.

"Fuck, Jessie. You must be trying to kill me."

"No," I said quite seriously. "I'm trying to get you to fuck me." I'd never been so brazen in my life, but it felt good. Really good. After all, I was doing this. Playing this sexy, dangerous game that I still couldn't quite believe. I might as well go all in. And dammit if I didn't want to. I'd played by the rules my whole life. I didn't take chances, I didn't put myself out there, I lived like a nun, and I was so very over it.

Dax moved quickly. He stripped his leather riding gloves off and tossed them to the ground before one hand found my breast. He squeezed and used his thumb to push the fabric of the bra down to get access to my nipple. His other hand laced through my hair, and he pulled me up so my mouth met his.

He kissed me with a deep hunger. My need for him grew stronger, if it were even possible. I was greedy. I wanted his hands all over me, his mouth on my skin, my tits—everywhere —I wanted his cock inside me. I craved it.

As if he read my mind, his hand left my breast and traveled to my upper thigh. He grazed my clit with his thumb before he gripped my leg and swung it over the bike. If his hand wasn't still on my head, pressing me tight to his lips, I might have slipped, but I wasn't worried. Dax had it under control. He had *me* under control.

His tongue possessed my mouth, taking everything he wanted. I completely lost myself in his kiss until his hand wrapped tightly in my hair and tugged my head back to expose my neck. I moaned with the slight wince of pain that only fueled my desire.

Dax's lips traveled down my neck, nipping and sucking, until he got to my breasts. He growled and gave each one a love bite in turn before moving farther south to my navel and finally my dripping wet pussy.

I wiggled my hips, needing more, but not even knowing what it was I needed. I was woefully inexperienced. Never had a man touched me the way Dax was. Never had a man put his mouth where Dax was no doubt about to. By reflex, I wiggled to move away but he held my hips firm so I couldn't move.

It was an exquisite torture as he knelt on the ground before me, tore the tiny scrap of silk from my body, and plunged his tongue inside me. I gasped. My hands grasped for something to hold on to. His tongue swirled and licked and lapped against my clit relentlessly. It was too much. So intense. I needed to move, but he held me fast. And then...I needed to come. Hard.

He must have sensed it, because seconds before I exploded, he moved away, leaving me almost sobbing, I was so desperate for the release only he would be able to give me.

"Not so fast, sweetheart." Dax stood in front of me, his hands working at the old leather belt of his jeans. "You'll come when I'm ready for you to come."

Somehow, I managed to sit on the bike, my body coiled tight and my chest heaving with deep pants. I was completely unable to catch my breath as he unzipped his jeans and let them fall to his feet, releasing his impossibly hard cock. It was huge. I licked my lips, and Dax growled again.

"I'm going to fuck you now."

I couldn't form words, but somehow, I managed a nod.

"Do you want that, sweetheart?"

Fuck, did I ever, but I still couldn't find my voice. I bit my bottom lip and nodded again, unable to take my eyes off his enormous cock.

It was overwhelming.

All of it.

The motorcycle. The push-up bra. The scrap of silk that was now destroyed. My nakedness. The exposed highway and the star-studded sky overhead. The overwhelming desire coursing through me made it impossible to think. The need for release that had quite literally taken away my ability to speak.

He took a step toward me, and a full-body shiver tore through me in anticipation of what was to come. But instead of pressing that impressive dick inside me, he took my chin in one hand and gripped it firmly, so I stared into his eyes.

"You need to stop it, Jessie."

Stop what? I swallowed hard.

"That's exactly what you're doing, isn't it?"

I nodded but I didn't understand what he was talking about. Not really.

"You need to get out of your head."

Okay. That I could understand. I had a terrible habit of overthinking things to the point of frustration.

"Do you want me to fuck you?"

I tried to nod, but he held my head firm.

"I need to hear you say it."

"Yes." My voice came out as a small squeak. "Please."

His nostrils flared. "I want to do that more than anything," Dax said. "But I need you to get out of your head if you're going to be able to completely let go."

My chest heaved with each breath I took; my breasts strained so hard against the confines of the bra, it was almost painful.

"Do you trust me, Jessie?"

I nodded without hesitation because I did. Implicitly.

"Say it."

"I trust you, Dax."

Without further hesitation, Dax grabbed my hip and spun me around. He pressed one hand on my back, pushing me into the seat of the motorcycle until my ass was lifted in the air.

"Remember rule number one?"

Puzzled, I tried to turn my head to see what he was talking about. But before I could, the palm of his hand came down with a sharp sting and the sound reverberated through the night air. The combination of pleasure with the slightest bit of pain only amplified my excitement. *Rule one: hold on.* I gripped the bike with one hand and instinctively reached around to try to cover my bare ass.

Dax's hand dipped between my legs to feel the juices that were now dripping down my legs.

"You liked that, didn't you?"

Despite myself, I nodded.

"Tell me, sweetheart. Tell me how you like letting go of control."

His words, delivered with rough need laced through his voice, almost put me over the edge.

You need to get out of your head. Stop overthinking.

It made perfect sense. *Do you trust me?*

My whole life I'd been in control of everything. Every detail. Letting go of control had never been an option. Overthinking and being in my head had been a way to get through the day. I swallowed hard and, with complete honesty, said, "I like it so much, Dax. I like letting go of control."

I hadn't planned to give her a spanking, but dammit, she was all up in her head, and I could see that she wouldn't be able to enjoy everything I planned to do with her until she shut off her brain a little. I didn't know enough of her background. But I didn't have to. A single mom with her own business who'd had to keep it all together. It didn't take a genius to see that she'd spent far too long controlling every single fucking detail of her life. More than anything in my whole life, I wanted to be inside the warm heat of her, but only if I could get her to let go a little first. I needed her to be all in on this. One hundred percent. And I knew enough to know there was one way for a woman as tightly controlled as Jessie to let go.

And I'd been right.

Her response had been immediate.

I like letting go of control.

So. Fucking. Hot.

Slowly, I rubbed my hand over the hot red mark my first slap had left behind. She moaned a little and relaxed into it. So, I delivered another one.

Jessie tried to swallow the little shriek of surprise when my skin connected with hers.

"Let it out, sweetheart. Let it go."

Without hesitation, I delivered two more. This time she didn't try to stifle her cry.

When I reached between her legs, they came back dripping with her juices. Every spank I landed only made her hotter. I pushed my finger inside her wet heat, and she groaned against me.

The process of her releasing herself to me and giving me control of her pleasure was almost enough to be my own undoing.

It hadn't taken much, but it had been necessary, and I knew now she was ready.

And more to the point, my cock was straining to slide into her wet pussy. I'd waited long enough.

I rubbed my hand over her flaming-hot skin. The heat coming off her ass was enough that I knew she wouldn't be able to sit down all day without remembering how she'd relinquished her control to me. *Perfect. She'd be thinking of me all day. She'd be wet for me all day.*

The thought only made me need her more.

I pressed my lips to each sensitive ass cheek in turn before pulling a condom out of my vest and sheathing myself. I slid my throbbing cock along the swell of her perfect ass cheeks before nudging the tip to her wet pussy lips.

"Do you want me to fuck you now?"

"More than anything."

That was all I needed. I held tight to her hips and, with one thrust, pushed into her.

Fuck. She was tight and perfect. Her pussy clamped down around me, taking all of me.

Beneath me, Jessie groaned, and her hips came back to meet me, greedy for more. She groaned, but I couldn't make out the words.

I twisted her hair around my fingers and pulled her head back. "What was that, sweetheart?"

Her lips came up in a sexy grin and she repeated herself. "Fuck me, Dax," she said. "Fuck me hard."

And that's just what I did.

Harder, deeper with every thrust so she had to hold on to the bike seat. Until I could feel her tighten around me as her climax began to roll over her. It was enough to send me over the top, too.

When her orgasm hit, Jessie screamed out into the dark

night, and I roared out my own release as I filled her. She collapsed, spent, over the bike.

With one hand holding her, I quickly pulled up my jeans before I scooped her into my arms. She wrapped her arms around my neck so her magnificent breasts pressed into my chest. I leaned against the bike and held her close.

She was fucking amazing. Everything about her.

And she didn't even know who I was.

Chapter Nine

IT HAD BEEN JUST over two weeks since I'd first met my mysterious sexy biker Dax and it had easily been the best weeks of my life. Sure, I was getting even less sleep than I usually did, but it didn't matter because I was being fueled with amazing sex and—it was crazy to even think about it, but—maybe even *love*.

It was completely insane that I was even thinking that way, but I couldn't help it. Because it felt like more than just sex. Although, that *was* amazing, and I was definitely not complaining about our nightly rendezvous. In such a short time, I'd had better sex than the whole of my entire life.

But it was more than that, too. He was so thoughtful and considerate of me, remembering details from our conversations and every single day, he made me feel important and special. It seemed silly, but every morning I'd wake up to a text of a cute graphic that said, "Good morning, beautiful." Or "Have a great day!" Or something equally sweet. It made me feel like a teenager and made my stomach flip every time I picked up my phone first thing in the morning to see it.

And it wasn't just cute text messages, either. After we'd

been seeing each other about a week, a used Toyota showed up at Rosie's with a note.

Jessie,
   I'm not using it right now.
   Drive safe. Dax

There was no way I could accept the gift of a car. Not when I had no hope in paying it back, and that's exactly what I told Dax when he arrived at Rosie's later that night.

"It's not a gift," he said as I poured him his usual cup of coffee. "It's a loaner. Just until you have time to find something of your own."

"Dax. I can't take your car."

"I'm not using it." He pointed in the direction of the motorcycle outside. "I have the bike. Besides," he flashed me that sexy smile that made me melt, "I couldn't live with myself if anything happened to you taking the bus or walking home late at night. Not when I had a perfectly good car that I wasn't using."

We both knew that as long as he was showing up on his motorcycle to drive me home, nothing would happen to me. Nothing I didn't want, anyway. My imagination flared with naughty thoughts.

But I was brought back into the moment with Dax gripping my hand. "Please, Jessie. Borrow the car. It's not anything special. But it will get you around safely."

I relented, but only temporarily. I made sure that it was a loan and not a gift. I'd buy myself a new car just as soon as I had a minute. And some spare cash.

After I'd accepted the *loan* of the car, Dax and I fell into a rhythm where he would show up at the diner about an hour before closing. He always sat in the same booth where we could sneak some kisses or quick inappropriate touches. I felt like a teenager again. Or more specifically, I felt like I *should* have felt when I was a teenager if I hadn't been dating Barrett who, in hindsight, didn't seem attracted to me at all. Not the way Dax was. As if he couldn't keep his hands off me. And he couldn't.

It was intoxicating. But it wasn't just the sex. It was the conversation and the way we were getting to know each other. It hardly seemed possible that it had only been such a short time.

On the slow nights at the diner—of which there were more and more—I'd sit with him and we'd talk and flirt as if we were on a real date.

"Your kids sound great," he said.

"They are." I lit up the way I always did when I talked about the kids. "I don't want to sound like they're angels," I added. "We definitely had our share of rough times, late nights and tears. Theirs and mine."

"I imagine." Dax nodded thoughtfully. "Raising kids on your own can't be easy."

"It wasn't. But I wouldn't trade it for anything." I sipped my coffee. "What about you? You never wanted kids?"

I was worried he would shut down at the question, but instead he simply shrugged. "Maybe once," he answered honestly. "I was married very briefly about fifteen years ago."

It was the first time he'd mentioned an ex-wife. I tried not to look too surprised so he'd keep talking.

"The idea of kids crossed my mind back then, but to be honest, the marriage didn't last long enough for it to ever be a real consideration."

"What happened?"

He shrugged again. "It just didn't work out."

He looked down and I got the idea that the subject was closed, which was fine with me. After all, fifteen years was a long time and I didn't like talking about my ex either.

We moved on to other subjects, and each night I learned a

little more. I learned that he'd gone to college but didn't use his education. He didn't like to talk about his work much, only that it was a means to an end, whatever that meant.

He was the only child of parents who were still happily married. He told me that he was largely a workaholic, but I had a hard time visualizing that considering I got the impression he wasn't very good at sales. At least not based on the worn-out jeans and T-shirts he always wore with his leather biking vest. Every time I pressed him on it, he changed the subject and really, I could respect the fact that he didn't like to talk about work. We talked about so many other things anyway.

And everything I learned about him, I loved.

Loved.

I couldn't stop myself from thinking that way. Even though it hadn't been very long since we'd been seeing each other, it felt like it had been months. Years even. Our conversations grew deeper and deeper, and it didn't take long for me to think of Dax as a fixture in my life. It was crazy to think that we could possibly be building a relationship that started on the back of a motorcycle. But we were. He'd woken something inside me.

And, for the first time, I started to believe that maybe a happily ever after *was* possible.

I was getting in too deep and I knew it. But knowing something and giving a shit were two very different things. And I didn't give a shit that Jessie was occupying more and more of my waking thoughts.

And my sleeping thoughts.

Not that I was sleeping much. Between the late nights at the diner followed by our sexy rendezvous after Jessie closed up, I wasn't getting back to my apartment until well after two in the morning. Getting up at six to be at the office was getting harder and harder.

It was worth it.

What had started as a simple way to blow off some steam had morphed very quickly into more. So much more. Because Jessie was more. She was easy to talk to, and I found myself telling her all about my childhood, my friends, college, and more. Leaving out any of the details that would give away my identity, of course. I still wasn't ready to tell her the truth. It was too soon.

Too soon for what?

I found myself thinking that way more and more. As if Jessie was more than just a way to blow off steam. And I still wasn't convinced. Sure, I enjoyed spending time with her—and not just for the sex, although that was pretty amazing—but I genuinely *liked* her.

It might have been a mistake giving her the car so soon, but I couldn't stop myself. There was no way I could be okay knowing that I had the means to help her out and she was taking the bus or walking around when there was no need for it.

But finding her an appropriate car was a bit of a challenge. When I gave Kenny the instructions to source a reliable used car that had a few dents or scratches in the paint, he'd looked at me as if I'd lost my mind.

Maybe I had.

But I couldn't give her a brand-new car. She would never accept it, and she'd start to suspect that maybe I wasn't telling her everything about who I really was. And I couldn't have that, because I'd tell her when I was ready. *If* I was ready.

For now, I was going to enjoy the time we were spending together. And if it meant keeping my secret a little bit longer while I drank strong coffee every night, I would.

Every night after I closed the diner, we'd get on the back of Dax's bike and ride. Sometimes it was a longer ride; sometimes it was really short. But every single night we'd end up in what I was quickly coming to think of as *our spot* by the river, where we'd fool around. Most of the time, he'd fuck me until I couldn't think straight. But sometimes we'd tease each other and fool around a little bit, making out like teenagers and continuing our conversations from earlier.

I'd invited him back to my house twice, but each time he'd refused, so I stopped asking. Not that it mattered. We didn't need a bed. The sex we had on his bike, or on a blanket he would lay down in the grass, was everything and so much more than I ever thought I needed.

He knew how to draw me out and make me feel things I'd never felt before. And man, did I ever feel them.

"I'm totally falling for him." I finished filling in Abby, Sandy, and Darla, who'd joined me at my kitchen table for a coffee instead of our usual drinks at Rosie's. Brittany had begged off with some sort of lame work excuse. We were used to her bailing because of work, but I got a weird vibe from her when she'd called to tell me she couldn't make it. Maybe she just wasn't in the mood to hear about another of her friends finding love.

Love.

There was that word again.

"Do you think that Britt didn't come today because she's afraid we'll push her into the pact next?" The idea hit me out of the blue. "I mean, I don't want her to feel—"

"I'm sure she's just super busy with work." Abby interrupted me. "Don't worry about it," she added. "It'll be her turn soon, whether she likes it or not."

"Besides," Sandy said. "I really do think she's crazy at work right now. She mentioned something about another merger. She works too hard."

She did. We all thought so. Still, I couldn't help but think she was avoiding me. I hadn't heard from her much since I started dating Dax.

"So," Abby said. "You're falling for him…" She brought the conversation back around. "What does that mean exactly?"

"Please don't say love." Darla groaned. "It's too soon."

"It's not." I shook my head. "I mean, normally I would agree with you, but this is…it's just so different than anything I've ever felt before. He's so sweet and attentive and yet, manly and sexy and all the things all at the same time. Besides, it's not like we're twenty anymore, right? I mean, there's no rules about waiting a set amount of time before feeling the feelings, is there?"

"There's not," Abby agreed. "I think that's one of the best parts of being over forty. Do you, girl. There are no rules."

It felt so good to share everything with my girlfriends. It made it all feel more real, like I wasn't just dreaming this incredibly sexy man who was super into me.

"I have to admit," Sandy said. "It sure sounds good." She propped her chin up on her hand and all but sighed like a dreamy teenager. "I'll be the first to admit that I wasn't super excited about this whole pact thing. But…it really does seem to be working out for you, Jessie. And that look in your eyes." She did sigh then. "That's how it was for me once. It feels like a million years ago."

"With Greg?" Darla asked. "I don't remember you being all lovestruck like this."

Sandy shot up in her chair, her mouth making a circle. "Of course, with Greg. There's never been anyone else. You know that."

I looked between Sandy and the rest of my friends, and back to Sandy. As far as I knew, there hadn't been anyone else.

Unless someone knew something I didn't, which by the looks of it, they didn't.

Everyone shook their heads and Darla finally shrugged. "Sorry. I didn't…"

"It's fine." Sandy brushed it away, as if she hadn't just looked as though she'd seen a ghost. "So," she changed the subject, "what's next for you guys? Do you think you'll introduce him to the kids?"

It was my turn to look surprised. *The kids.* Of course. "I mean…I guess…I…of course I—"

"It's still pretty new," Abby interrupted. "Give her a chance to figure it out."

I gave Abby a grateful look.

She winked and then added, "Seems to me you have at least one thing figured out pretty well, though. The sex sounds—"

"Fantastic." I couldn't help but squeal. "We do things I never thought I'd…" I trailed off, unsure whether I should tell them about the spanking Dax had given me the first night we'd been together. I still couldn't believe I'd not only *let* him do that but that I'd enjoyed it. A lot. He was right; I was so caught up in my head and overthinking everything, I probably would never have been able to let myself enjoy what was happening. At least not as much as I had. He just seemed to know both what my body and my mind needed to get the most pleasure.

"What?" Abby pushed, clearly noticing there was something I wasn't saying. "What did you do?" Her eyes were wide with interest, so I took a deep breath and told them.

"Really?" When I was finished telling them all the details, Sandy shook her head in disbelief. "I mean, I don't doubt that you did…I mean, I've read books with…I'm not a total prude."

"No one is calling you a prude," I said.

"I kind of am." Darla laughed. "Just kidding," she said to

Sandy before turning back to me. "But seriously, I'm so glad for you that you're exploring all these things. Sex is supposed to be fun and adventurous and exciting. It's about bloody time you're figuring that out."

"Right?" I sighed deeply and leaned back against my chair. "It's hard to even describe how it feels when you finally have good sex."

"I wouldn't know." Darla laughed. "I mean, it's always been fabulous for me."

"But really," Abby put her mug down and looked at Darla, "don't you think it would be better if it was with someone you cared about?"

Darla almost spat out her coffee. "Seriously? Please don't tell me you buy into that bullshit."

Abby shrugged.

Darla nodded and she didn't even bother looking at me, because I'd just finished telling them all how I thought I was falling in love with my sex god.

"You guys are serious?"

"Totally," Abby said. "I mean, don't get me wrong. Sex is almost always pretty good. But when it's with someone you really care about *and* connect with that way, it's just…mmm."

I laughed, because she was one hundred percent correct.

"And you had that with Greg, Sandy? You loved him *and* connected with him in a fireworks kind of way?"

Sandy looked down quickly and picked up her mug to take a deep sip before finally answering. "We're not talking about me."

I raised my eyebrows and looked at Abby. We'd circle back to *that* comment at a later date.

Darla shook her head and topped up her coffee from the pot I'd left on the table. "Well, we're not talking about me either. We're talking about you, Jessie." She lifted her mug in a cheers toward me. "So besides super sexy biker man, what else is going on? Why aren't we meeting at the diner tonight?"

Instinctively I looked down. I didn't want to lie to my friends, but I also didn't want to bring the mood down. The truth was, being in the diner was starting to bring *my* mood down. Despite the sudden short-lived burst of new customers who clearly were only interested in gawking at my giant breasts but realized I wasn't interested in anything more than serving them coffee and maybe a burger if they weren't too cheap to order food, it wasn't enough to change the bottom line. I'd run the numbers a million different ways and they weren't getting any better. If things didn't change, and soon, I'd lose Rosie's.

Or I'd be forced to take the offer that I still wasn't convinced was enough.

"What's going on, Jessie?" Abby was up and out of her chair, a hand on my back. "Is everything okay? The kids, are they—"

"It's the diner." I blurted it out before I could change my mind. "I'm going to lose it."

"What?"

"Why?"

"Tell us everything."

This was it. At least it *should* be it.

After this meeting, a few dozen signed documents, lots of handshaking and fake smiles, followed by a celebratory dinner where there would be too much wine and not nearly enough whiskey to get me through it, it would be done. The merger would be official, and everything would calm down again. I'd no longer need the stress release every night to keep me from imploding at the office the next day.

I could go back to normal. Working twelve-hour days,

followed by dinners at the club, drinks with colleagues or old friends, with the occasional long bike rides to blow off steam. Mixed in with regular sexual releases with a random woman whose name I either didn't know or wouldn't remember in the morning.

Normal.

The way I'd been doing things for years. Decades, really. It worked for me. I was successful. I had everything I needed, without any messy personal attachments. I'd tried that with Courtney. It hadn't worked. I liked things better this way. Simple. Clean.

In the morning, the deal would be done and my affair with Jessie would be finished.

The only problem was, I wasn't sure I wanted it to be finished.

I took another look around the boardroom, at the faces of my employees and colleagues who were working hard to button up this deal so we could all move on. They'd been working around the clock to make sure all the details were taken care of and nothing slipped through the cracks. I didn't know anybody who worked harder than these people. Except for myself.

Usually.

The truth was I'd been sitting in that boardroom for at least ninety minutes already and if pressed, I wouldn't be able to contribute anything of value to the conversation because I had no idea what anyone was talking about. I hadn't been listening.

While I was nodding and pretending to give a fuck about buying up this software, truthfully, all I could think about was Jessie in the pink bra and panties set I'd given her a few days earlier. It became clear quite quickly that she enjoyed the lingerie, and considering I also very much enjoyed it, I ordered her five more sets with extra panties—since I'd developed a bad habit of tearing them off her.

So far, I couldn't decide whether I liked the soft pink that blended in almost perfectly with her diner uniform so it almost looked as if she were naked under the thin cotton, or whether I liked the emerald green that made her eyes sparkle and her dark hair shine.

Who was I trying to fool? I liked them all.

"Is something funny, Shane?"

My head snapped up to see my CFO, who also happened to be one of Jessie's best friends, watching me with narrowed eyes. "Sorry?"

"You laughed."

I did?

I'd been so lost in my daydream fantasies of Jessie, I didn't even notice.

"Sorry," I said with a shake of my head. "I didn't realize."

"I noticed." There was a challenge in Brittany's voice and when she didn't look away after a moment, I knew there was likely something more going on.

"Maybe we should take a ten-minute break," I suggested, but it was more like a command. "I think we could all use a little air to clear our heads."

My team didn't need to be told twice. Seconds later, folders snapped shut and chairs pushed back as everyone cleared out. Everyone except Brittany Donahue. I waited until the door swung shut behind Kenny, who looked at me in question. I'd dismissed him with a wave of my hand.

"Do you want to tell me what the problem is?" I asked point-blank. "Because something tells me that the way you're looking at me has nothing to do with the merger and everything to do with—"

"Don't say it."

"Don't say what?"

She pushed up from her chair and stalked to the end of the boardroom. "Don't say that this has everything to do with a certain sexy brunette that you're fucking."

I didn't even try to hide my shock. The crass choice of words took me aback. Sure, I'd thought them. Hell, I'd *said* them. Still… "You think I'd say that? To you? That I would refer to Jessie as a sexy brunette that I'm *fucking*?"

She spun around and put her hands on her hips. "Well, you are, aren't you?"

"Without a doubt." I sat back and crossed my arms over my chest. "Jessie is the sexiest brunette I've ever laid eyes on. And yes, I am in fact *fucking* her. But I wasn't going to refer to her that way," I continued. "As if she were just another conquest."

Brittany tilted her head. "Isn't she?"

"No." My answer was instantaneous, surprising both of us.

She opened her mouth and shut it again before turning away to look out the window, which was a good thing because I needed a moment to compose myself.

I had basically just admitted out loud to another person that Jessie was more to me than just another warm body, and I wasn't sure how to feel about that. Any other time, that admission would have scared the hell out of me. *But now…*

"No," I said again, this time with authority. I waited for Brittany to turn around. "I can't say what or who exactly Jessie is to me right now because, well, quite honestly, I'm still trying to figure that out myself. But I can say this with one hundred percent conviction. She is something special. And a whole lot more to me than any other woman has ever been." I nodded to myself, because that felt right. "Much more."

Brittany didn't say anything for a minute. Instead, she moved back to her seat and poured herself a glass of water. She took a small sip before slowly and deliberately replacing the glass on the table. Finally, she straightened. "Shane, I've worked for you for a while now and while I'm never going to claim to be a close friend, I do think I've seen enough to know that you don't have the best reputation with women. In fact," she continued before I could interrupt, "I've actually always been able to understand your approach to dating." She shrugged. "It's not too dissimilar to my own." She paused and picked up her water glass again. "And that's what worries me," she said before she took another sip. "Jessie is one of my best friends."

"I know."

"And if whatever it is you're doing with her is different in any way than what you usually do, what does that mean for her?"

I tilted my head in question and waited while she drank.

"She doesn't even know your real name, *Dax.*" She emphasized my pseudonym. "She doesn't know what you do for a living." Her voice rose a little. "And from what I understand," she said, "the entirety of your *relationship*"—I didn't like the emphasis she put on that word—"has involved screwing on the back of your motorcycle on the side of the highway."

I took a deep breath.

"So," Brittany continued. "I know exactly why it's different for her. And honestly, I'm missing a girl chat right now where no doubt everyone is hearing about exactly how she's feeling about all this. But forgive me, I'm not really seeing how any of this is different for you."

Her words hit me in the chest. I should be pissed that an employee, even a high ranking one, would speak to me so candidly, but I wasn't. Quite the opposite. Instead, I swallowed hard and thought about what she'd said.

I couldn't put it into words, but I didn't need to. I *felt* it. And the only thing that mattered now was that Jessie felt it, too.

Chapter Ten

BY THE TIME I filled the girls in on the offer I was going to have to be forced to accept because it was better than the alternative, I was exhausted. The girls gave me hugs and offers to do everything they could to help. Abby promised to talk to her fiancé, Phillip, and help me out with a lawyer to fight for a fair deal, if that's what it came to with the takeover deal. I managed to will myself to keep my emotions in check until after they left, and I closed the door behind them.

But by then I was out of energy completely. I poured myself another cup of coffee. I was going to need the caffeine if I was going to get through my shift later. Especially considering I didn't have a visit with Dax to look forward to. He'd said something about being out of town for work or something. Maybe it was the turn in my mood after talking about the diner, but suddenly his excuse for a work trip seemed a little suspicious. He *had* been vague about where he was going, and he still hadn't told me what it was he sold. *Was he really out of town? What if—*

No. Jessie, stop it!

I needed to stop letting my imagination get away from me.

Everything was fine. I needed to assume it was. Especially because he hadn't given me any reason to think otherwise.

I busied myself cleaning up the mugs and right before I hopped in the shower to start getting ready to head to the diner, my phone chimed with an incoming text.

Dax.

Instantly, a smile crossed my face and my body vibrated with the thought of him. Maybe it was a good thing that we were taking a night off from each other. My body was *very* out of practice with all the physical activity it had been getting, and muscles I didn't even know I had were sore.

I've been thinking about you, sweetheart.

I blushed the way I always did when he used my pet name. I'd never had one before and it made me feel special.

You have? What have you been thinking about?

I knew the answer before he typed it. Still, a series of very dirty texts followed that had me blushing and completely distracted from the task of getting ready for work.

You have to stop, or I'll never be able to get to work.

I quickly typed in my response because it was true. I would way rather spend the rest of the day in my bed fantasizing about him. It was second only to spending my day in bed *with* him. But since he was in…where *did* he go for his trip? He hadn't told me. Before he could respond to my last text, I quickly added more.

Where did you say you were going again?

He didn't respond for a moment. Finally, I heard the ding.

I didn't.

Now he really was being sketchy. My heart sank. Maybe I'd let myself believe too soon that Dax and I could have a real connection. *No doubt he was married with a family somewhere and I was just a—*

It's not important.

But it was. It was very important. And in that instant, my

mind went wild with the possibilities of why exactly Dax didn't feel it was important to tell me where he was. Was it because *I* wasn't important? Or maybe I just wasn't as important as I thought I was. Which was ridiculous, because we'd only been seeing each other for just over a few weeks. It wasn't like it was a relationship or anything. We were having sex. That was it. *Right?*

Ugh. This was exactly why I didn't date. I had no idea how to do it, and I just made an idiot of myself.

I left my phone on the bathroom counter, unable to respond in a way that wouldn't make me feel even more pathetic than I already felt. Less than an hour ago, I was on top of the world, telling my girlfriends about how magical things were with Dax and now...

I needed to stop overthinking it.

I let the shower run hot and steamy and stepped under the water, where I let it run over me for a few minutes, eyes closed and head tilted back. I was vaguely aware of my phone sitting silent on the countertop. He hadn't texted again. *The one time I let myself believe I might actually be lucky enough to—*

My negative train of thought was cut off by the sharp ring of my phone. With shampoo suds still in my hair, I was unable to help it when I popped my head around the curtain to see who it was.

Dax.

He was calling?

We'd never spoken on the phone. It felt oddly intimate, which was ridiculous considering what we had done together.

Still.

I left the water running, stepped out of the shower, and wrapped myself in a towel with my soapy hair dripping down my back. My voice shook as I answered the call.

"Hello?"

"You didn't text back." His voice was deep. Straight to the point. "Why?"

What could I say? That if it wasn't important to tell me where he was that it made me feel unimportant, too?

"I didn't know what to say," I answered honestly.

There was a deep silence and then a sigh. "I'm sorry," Dax said. "I'm not out of town at all. I'm stuck at the office. But I didn't want to tell you because I didn't want you to think I was choosing not to see you, Jessie."

That was definitely not the response I was expecting. But it also didn't make much sense. We only ever saw each other way after business hours. What kind of business was Dax really in that he'd have to work well into the night?

Alarm bells were ringing in my head but at the same time, I couldn't make myself hang up on him.

"You're probably wondering what I'm doing that I can't get away."

I was.

"I promise it's important business. And I want you to know that normally work would never keep me away from you. *Nothing* could keep me away from you, Jessie."

A shot of desire tore through me.

He sighed heavily. "Except this."

"It must be an important meeting."

"It is. But not as important as you. Say the word and I'll leave right now. I'll pick you up and—"

"No." I couldn't help the smile that crossed my face at the thought of my big, tough biker who would drop everything if I asked. *Wow.* "Don't leave. Work is important. But…"

"But what? Say the word, sweetheart. What do you want? I'll make it up to you. Anything."

I didn't even have to think about it. "A date," I said. "A real one."

He was silent for a minute, and I was afraid I might have asked for too much too soon. But that was stupid. Of course it wasn't too much to ask for a real date instead of dirty sex on the side of the highway. Although I had to admit, I liked that too. But my conversation with the girls and now this crazy conversation with Dax and the jumble of feelings I was having made one thing clear—I needed more from him. At least until I could figure out what it was.

"You want to go out?"

I nodded. "I do."

"And that would make you happy?"

Again, I nodded despite the fact he couldn't see me. "It would."

"I'll pick you up tomorrow night at seven."

"Really?"

He laughed. "Of course. I want to make you happy, Jessie. And you're right, we haven't gone out properly yet. I mean, I quite enjoy seeing you at the diner," he added. "But I could do with a break from your coffee."

"Hey," I protested with a laugh.

"There's nothing I'd like more than to take you out properly."

I could hear in his voice that he meant it.

"I'm sorry I haven't asked before, Jessie. I'm going to make up for it tomorrow. I promise you it will be the best date you've ever been on."

I laughed, because any date with him would without a doubt be the very best one I'd ever been on.

"It doesn't have to be fancy," I said. "I just…" I took a deep breath and decided to just go for it. No point in holding anything back. "Well," I tried again. "I know it hasn't been very long, Dax, but I really like spending time with you, and I think a date would be the next step."

I squeezed my eyes shut, thankful he couldn't see my face. I was so bad at this whole dating thing. I'd just made a monumental fool of myself. If I could melt into the bathroom floor, I would have. Happily.

"Jessie," he said after a moment. "I really like spending time with you, too."

I could hear the humor in his voice and it instantly made me feel better.

"A date is the exact right next step."

His answer was perfect. I wanted to dance around the bathroom and squeal like a teenager but somehow, I contained myself.

"What's the noise in the background?" Dax asked. "Is that the shower?"

"Yes. I was just rinsing my hair when you called, so I—"

"You're wet and naked right now?" His voice was gruff and full of need.

"I am."

"Dammit." The word came out as a groan. "I'm going to hang up now," he said after a moment. "Otherwise, there is no way I'm going to be able to concentrate on anything other than your tits with water streaming off them and—"

The call disconnected and then I did squeal like a teenage girl because I couldn't remember a time I'd ever been so happy.

She wanted to go out on a proper date. I hung up the phone and stared at it long after the screen went black.

For the first time in years, the idea of a real date, especially one with a woman I actually enjoyed, filled me with joy instead of dread. I couldn't think of anything I'd like more than going out with her.

Most importantly, it would make her happy, and with every

cell in my whole body, the only thing I wanted in the world was to make Jessie happy.

Damn.

And if that wasn't an indication that this woman was getting under my skin, I'm not sure what was.

The date had to be special. More than special. It had to be perfect.

But that was a problem because I had no idea how to date, let alone how to make a date perfect. I glanced around. My eyes landed first on Kenny, who was always nearby. He really was the best assistant and would do everything in his power—which, when paired with my credit card, was substantial—to work just the right magic. But it wouldn't be enough. I turned where I stood, and my eyes landed on Brittany.

Yes.

Sure, she was suspicious of me and my intentions with her friend; she'd made that much perfectly clear. But that was more the reason why it was perfect. Brittany would know exactly how to make it an amazing date and more importantly, she'd want it to be amazing.

"Brittany!"

She jumped at my bellow, but quickly composed herself.

She held her leather portfolio against her chest and walked slowly toward me. "I didn't realize it was time for the next meeting."

"It's not." I glanced at my watch but didn't really look at it. Suddenly I didn't care about the stupid merger. It wasn't important. Not like Jessie. "But I need your help."

Instantly, she narrowed her eyes. "Jessie?" She shook her head and started to back away. "I don't want to get involved in this, Shane. Not anymore than I already am. It's bad enough that I..." She gestured between the two of us. "I don't like lying to my friend. And not telling her who you are, well...I agreed not to, but—"

"No, no." I stopped her before she could talk herself into telling Jessie my name. I already knew that I'd tell her, but not yet. I needed this first. And then... "It's not like that, Brittany. This will only be a good thing for Jessie. And I do appreciate you keeping my secret for a little bit longer. I promise you there's a very good reason I'm keeping my identity from her, and it won't be much longer."

She eyed me.

"Really," I said. "I'm going to tell her soon. I just need to know she feels the same way about me that I feel about her. I'm falling in love with her, and I don't want to mess it up."

There was no one more surprised by my words than I was, but as soon as they slipped out, I knew it was true. *Love.* Yes. It felt right. My shoulders pulled back and my chest puffed out as a face-splitting grin took over my face.

Brittany's face underwent a series of transformations, but finally she sighed, and the smallest trace of a smile formed on her lips. "Love, huh?"

I nodded. "Will you help me? I need to plan a date."

"A date?" She dropped her head and shook it, but finally she looked up. "I will. Against my better judgment, I will help you. But it's for Jessie. She deserves to be happy more than anyone else I know."

My smile grew wider, if it were even possible, and before she could change her mind, I grabbed her arm and pulled her into an empty office. "It's tomorrow night," I said without preamble. "What should I do?"

She looked at me as if I'd just grown another head. "You've been on dates before, Shane."

"No." I ran my hand over the scruff on my chin. "Not like this. I've taken *a date* to a party or event at the club, but not since my ex have I gone on a real date, and this is so much more important than that ever was. I can't screw it up. Where should I take her?"

She laughed.

It was not the response I was looking for.

"This is all very cute." She waved her hand in my direction. "I don't think I've ever seen you like this."

I lifted my hands in exasperation. I needed help, not laughter.

"Okay, okay." Brittany finally took pity on me. "I assume you're going to take her out for dinner?"

Of course. I nodded.

"I happen to know that Jessie really likes sushi but hardly ever has the chance to have it."

"Sushi. Easy. We'll go to Yama Goya."

Brittany agreed. "Get the private room. It's very romantic."

"And *private*." My groin tightened, thinking about what exactly we could get up to in that curtained room.

"I get it, you guys have a lot of sex." Brittany groaned. "It doesn't mean I want to hear about it. At least not from you. I already hear about it from her."

"You do?" The idea of Jessie telling all her friends about our sex life hadn't occurred to me. Not in a real sense. But I liked it. As long as she was saying good things. And I didn't even have to ask to know she was.

"Of course I do." Brittany shook her head. "But if you want this to be a romantic date," she continued, "you might want to focus on that part of the date, not the sex part."

"Really?" She might be right. It's not something I'd tried before, leading with romance. And it was definitely something different than what we'd already done together. A real date. "Okay," I agreed before she had to convince me.

"Pick her up in a car."

"What?" But Jessie liked the bike. *A lot.*

"A car," Brittany repeated. "If she's going to be wearing a pretty dress, the last thing she's going to want is to try to navigate a motorcycle seat."

I bit my tongue before telling her that Jessie didn't have any trouble navigating the motorcycle in a dress.

"And speaking of a dress," she continued. "Jessie won't have anything appropriate to wear, and that's going to stress her out."

That was the last thing I wanted. This was supposed to be fun and exciting, not stressful.

"I'll have someone sent to her house with a selection of—"

"Are you kidding?"

I wasn't.

"If you send a stylist with a rack of dresses that are all worth more than the car she no longer has, do you think she's going to believe whatever stupid story you've told her about who you are? Or do you think she's going to start to suspect that you're some sort of multi-billionaire?" Brittany tilted her head and narrowed her eyes in such a way that I laughed.

"Okay, you're right. So what do I—"

"I'll handle it. I know Jessie and her size."

"So do I." I knew every inch of her almost as well as I knew myself.

"I'm sure you do, but I've known Jessie for a very long time and I know exactly what she'll like."

It was a struggle to hand this particular task over to Brittany. So far, I'd only picked out lingerie for Jessie, but I'd made perfect selections. Still, she might have a point. I sighed. "Okay, but it has to be sexy. Sexier than she would choose for herself normally. She has no idea how gorgeous she really is."

Brittany gave me a look that made it clear she approved of that comment. "I got this. Red?"

"Definitely. But a deep, classy red."

"Of course."

"Shoes?"

"High," I said without hesitation. "Those legs deserve to be shown off." I'd done plenty of admiring of Jessie's legs, but I loved the idea of them on display, long and lean with heels instead of the sneakers she usually wore to the diner.

"I'll find something suitable. Anything else?"

I hesitated. Brittany was taking care of all the details, but there was one I could handle on my own. The lingerie. "No. I'll handle the rest."

"Okay. Got it." She finished scribbling something. Clicked her pen and gave me a grin. "You know you owe me a raise for this, right?"

She was joking, but she wasn't wrong.

"I do, Brittany. But not just for helping me out with this." I couldn't read her expression. "You have been indispensable to me and this company. Your work on this merger has been phenomenal. I'm very impressed, Brittany."

"Thank you, Shane. That means a lot." She pressed her lips together. "You know, my friends accuse me of working too much, but I really do love what I do. Thank you for trusting me with this position."

I nodded, because what else could I say? "Let's get back to work, shall we? The faster we finish up with this merger, the sooner we'll both have a bit more free time."

Somehow, I suffered through the rest of the meetings, only taking a few minutes to call the lingerie shop and arrange for a delivery. Shortly after, Brittany sent me a text message to let me know that she'd taken care of the details on her end. There was nothing left to do now but wait and somehow suffer through the next twenty-four hours until I could see Jessie again. I'd meant it when I told Brittany I'd tell Jessie the truth about who I was. I would. More than anything, I wanted her to know exactly who I was. But first I needed to be sure about how she felt about me. The real me. Not the super-wealthy businessman Shane Grant.

Although, if I were honest, it didn't even matter. Because I was already gone. If Jessie rejected me, it would destroy me because I'd already done the unthinkable. I'd let my guard down; I'd let her in. It had happened so fast I didn't even notice. In hindsight, it probably happened the first time I laid eyes on her. I was an intelligent man. I'd built an empire on well-thought-out, calculated decisions. I didn't believe in fate or love at first sight or any of that woo-woo bullshit.

Until now.

Chapter Eleven

MAYBE IT WAS a bad decision and maybe I should have cared more than I did, but given how slow business had been lately, I couldn't bring myself to pay Doris overtime to work the night shift so I could go on a proper date with Dax. So I taped the handwritten note to the door that we were closing early and had just flipped the lock when a sleek, black sports car that had no business being in the parking lot of my greasy spoon diner pulled into the parking lot.

I waited and watched with one hand on my hip and a bad feeling in my gut. A bad feeling that was confirmed the moment Trent Thomas unfolded his tall body from the front seat. He had an envelope in his hand.

The final offer.

I knew it would be coming soon. The Closed sign had gone up in the dry cleaner's window only a few days before, followed by the vacuum repair shop. They'd been the last holdouts.

It was only me left now. And I wasn't stupid enough to think that a big shot like Trent Thomas was going to let a woman and her run-down diner stand in the way of what was no doubt a development deal worth more money then I could even comprehend.

I watched for a moment and contemplated my choices. Not that I had many. But I had an important date in only a few hours. A date that I should be getting ready for and getting excited about. A conversation with Trent was definitely going to put a damper on that excitement.

Still.

I sighed. I couldn't avoid it forever.

But it didn't mean I had to roll out the welcome mat either. I watched the man closely as he walked up to the door. We stared at each other through the glass for a moment until I finally reached down, unlatched the lock, and turned to walk to the counter.

Behind me, I heard the jingle of the bells as Trent Thomas entered my diner.

"Closing early today, Jessie?"

I shrugged and turned around, a hand on my hip. "I have an appointment tonight."

He lifted his eyebrows. "An appointment?" Trent made a show of looking around my empty diner. "It wouldn't have anything to do with the fact that business has all but dried up, would it?"

My eyes narrowed into a glare. I crossed my arms over my body, which had the effect of pushing my breasts up further than they already were. It wasn't my intention, but I saw his gaze flicker quickly to my chest before once more meeting my eyes. "If business is slow," I said, keeping my voice icy and cold, "it's only because of you and your singular drive to ruin my business."

The smirk fell off his face in an instant and just like that, I actually saw a softer side of the man. A side I wouldn't have believed existed. "Jessie, that's really not what I'm trying to do," he said. "I hope you believe that."

The fight drained out of me. "It doesn't matter what I believe, Mr. Thomas. Does it?" I didn't wait for a reply. "I assume you're here today with another offer."

He nodded. "It's our final offer." He took a few steps toward me and extended his hand that held the envelope. "I need to tell you, this is as good as it's going to get, Jessie. Everyone else has sold. You're the only one left."

"Which means you need me." I felt a flicker of hope.

But he only shrugged. "Honestly?"

I nodded.

"I do want to be honest with you, Jessie, because I really do feel badly. You seem like a really nice woman and whether you believe it or not, this isn't personal and it's not about destroying you or your dreams. It's business."

I listened.

"We do need your land, yes. But I've been doing this for a while now and I can tell you from experience what will happen next. If you don't take the offer, which is a good one, I want to add—"

I glanced down at the envelope in my hand.

"The development will still go ahead. Permits will be applied for and in a town like Aspen Valley, they will be approved quickly. Soon, and it won't take very long, with no other supporting businesses here, you won't be able to sell enough coffee or pieces of pie to pay the bills. You'll end up shutting your doors anyway, only without a buyout. And if you're lucky and smart enough, you'll do that before you have to claim bankruptcy and truly have nothing. My company will come in and buy your property from the bank for a fraction of what we're offering you now, only you will have nothing to show for it." He nodded to the envelope. "Or you could make the best decision for you and your family and accept what I'm offering now."

His words hurt but there was no malice in them. I believed

everything he told me. And just as I predicted, I was out of options.

Still, I couldn't speak. And I couldn't bring myself to open the envelope. Not yet. Trent seemed to sense that I wasn't ready.

He nodded. "Take a bit of time, Jessie, and think it over. My contact information is in the envelope. If you decide to take me up on the offer, I'm currently working out of the offices of MultiTech Software. Shane Grant is an old friend of mine. Do you know of it?"

I'd heard the name, sure. Everyone had. Shane Grant was one of the wealthiest men in town. He was also Brittany's boss. I remembered how excited she'd been to land that job. Beyond that, I didn't know anything. Why would I? That wasn't my life, and I had more important things to worry about than the lifestyles of the rich and douchey. Which he undoubtedly was. *Weren't they all?* "I know where the offices are, yes," I said after a moment.

"Good. I'll be there tomorrow if you want to come by. Just shoot me a text."

"Tomorrow? But you said to take my——"

"A little friendly advice?" He didn't wait for my response. "Don't wait too long, Jessie."

———

"Did I catch you at a bad time, Mom?"

"No," I lied to Sadie and juggled the bags in my arm so I could open the front door with the phone tucked under my chin. "Not at all." I almost tripped over a stack of packages and narrowly caught myself before falling over. "What's up, kiddo?"

Okay, I probably shouldn't have answered the phone considering I only had just over an hour to get ready for my date with Dax. After Trent's appearance, I'd shoved the envelope into my purse and, determined to put the whole mess out of my mind at least for a night, I headed to the mall in hopes of finding something appropriate to wear on my date. I'd done three laps of the mall before I finally found a dress that wasn't terrible *and* didn't max out my credit card. It was much harder than I'd expected, considering I couldn't remember the last time I'd actually gone shopping.

I dutifully half listened with one ear while my daughter filled me in on life at college, including which professors were terrible and which would be pushovers. She told me all about the new friends she'd made. On any other day, I'd be excited to hear from her and want all the details, and the mom part of me felt immense guilt that I wasn't giving her all of my attention. But I was really pressed for time and—

I turned, remembering the packages I'd stepped over to get into the house, and went to retrieve them from the porch. Immediately my heart fluttered in my chest to see a familiar white box with a simple pink ribbon tied around it. The same packaging all the lingerie Dax had sent me had arrived in. *But what was the other two boxes?*

"Mom? Did you hear me?"

"What?" I shook my head and refocused. "I'm sorry, I was distracted. I just got a package and...honey, can I call you tomorrow? I actually have plans tonight and I should—"

"You have *plans?*"

I probably should have been a little offended at her reaction but instead I laughed.

"Mom? That's great!" Sadie squealed. "It's about time you got a life. And now that Lucas and I are gone, I'm so happy that you're not just sitting home alone."

If only she knew.

No.

My daughter definitely didn't need to know what I'd been up to.

I couldn't help but giggle a little.

"I won't keep you, Mom. Talk tomorrow, okay?"

"Of course. I'll call in the morning. I love you, kiddo."

She made a kissing noise into the phone and the call ended.

I gathered up the boxes and carefully took them to my bed, where I laid them out in a row. I was dying to open them. I was terrible at not leaving an unopened package, but I was running out of time and the last thing I wanted was to be unprepared when Dax showed up. The packages would still be there when I got out of the shower, and I knew that there was a very good chance that at least one of them contained the undergarments I would be wearing under the black dress I'd found at the last store I visited. There was nothing special about it. Long sleeves, a high neckline, and a hem that went below my knees, it didn't really do much for my shape but it was the best I could find. I really hoped Dax liked it. But then again, he seemed to like me in my uniform, so maybe the dress would be an improvement.

I would have liked a long, steamy shower, but because I was short on time, I rushed through and blow-dried my thick hair as fast as I could, a task that took way too much time. I finally slowed down so I could apply my makeup, something I hadn't done properly in a long time. Fortunately, I'd remembered the basics of eyeliner and mascara, and the new lip gloss I'd bought plumped up my lips nicely.

I took a step back and examined myself in the mirror.

Not bad.

And it hadn't taken nearly as long as I thought it might. Plenty of time to see what sexy underthings Dax sent me. He didn't strike me as a man who had a lot of money, so the fact he was sending me expensive lingerie had to mean he liked me. I felt like a teenager as I slid the box toward me and let my fingers run over the pink ribbon. I knew what would be in the box. My eyes drifted to the other two. But I had no idea what was in the others. Finally, curiosity got the best of me and before I could talk myself out of it, I tore open the smallest box.

Shoes.

But not just any shoes. The most beautiful shiny black leather heels I'd ever seen. I immediately slid my foot into one. It fit perfectly. And holy shit, was it high. I put the other one on and the effect was immediate. Even wrapped in only my towel, I looked instantly sexier. And about five inches higher.

I took a few steps, noticing how the height of the shoes pushed my hips out dramatically, causing my ass to sway from side to side. *Wow. There was a reason women wore shoes like this.* They were sexy as hell.

I went for the familiar lingerie box next, ready to don the bra and panties. But when I lifted the lid and moved the tissue paper aside, it was something different.

A corset.

I'd never worn anything like this silky garment. It was made of silk and black lace, with boning that would hug my body tight. The cups were smaller than the bras I'd been wearing and didn't look like they would contain my breasts fully. I'd never worn a corset before, but I knew enough to know they were designed to push your breasts impossibly high and narrow the waist into an hourglass shape. There were garter clips hanging from the bottom. I lifted it to look underneath, but there were no panties in the box, only some black thigh-high nylons. My nipples tightened to hard points, imagining what it would feel like on my skin. *If I could squeeze my body into it.* I wasn't completely convinced it was possible. But he hadn't been wrong on the sizing yet.

By the time I opened the third box, I had already guessed that I wouldn't be wearing my mall-bought dress.

But I wasn't at all ready for what I found inside.

The dress I pulled from the tissue was gorgeous.

And red.

I always wore black. I couldn't wear red. I shook my head at the beautiful dress and looked to the plastic bag that held the boring dress I'd purchased.

This red dress was a wrap style that would wind around me and tie at the side, revealing quite a bit of cleavage. It flared into a skirt that would land just over my knees, showing way more leg than I was used to.

There was no way I could wear it. And with the corset? There was no way.

But...there was only one way to find out.

I dropped my towel and took off my new shoes long enough to slide the nylons over my smooth legs. It took me a few minutes to figure out all the clips on the corset, but when I finally got it in place and stood in front of the mirror, I was stunned.

The lingerie nipped in my waist and just as I guessed, pushed up my tits to an almost impossible level, with the cups acting more like a shelf that just barely covered my nipples. My breasts were pushed together, two perfect creamy-white globes creating even more cleavage than the push-up bras had. I didn't think it was possible.

I'd never worn garter straps before, and I liked the way they pressed against my legs as I moved. Like a secret only I had. Without panties, my pussy was exposed, which I assumed was intentional, although I almost went to find a pair of panties. But the idea of not wearing any in public was thrilling, and that thought alone was enough to get me excited, as if the lingerie wasn't enough.

I still had my reservations as I lifted the silky red dress from the box and slipped into it. I tied it at my waist and to my surprise, it fit perfectly. Just as I expected, the cut of the top was low and with the corset pushing my breasts up, I had cleavage for days. The lingerie sucked me in in all the right places and the dress skimmed over my waist, giving me perfect definition and accenting my curves. I quickly stepped into the high heels and walked the length of the room and back as I watched in the mirror.

The skirt flounced and danced over my thighs as I walked, every once in a while affording a peek-a-boo look of the garter strap.

I'd never worn anything like it. It was both classy and sexy and made me feel like a completely different version of myself. And I liked it.

I grabbed my phone off the counter and snapped a picture of me in the mirror before quickly texting the group chat. The girls would not believe it.

Sure enough, the response was almost instant.

Jessie? Sandy responded first. *Holy shit, girl!*

Abby was next. *You look stunning!*

I couldn't help the squeal of delight that slipped from my lips. *Can you believe this? Dax sent me this dress. I've never worn anything like it.*

It's amazing. Darla's response. *You won't even make it to the restaurant looking like that.*

The thought had crossed my mind. Not that I'd mind. A night off from Dax and the pleasure he'd awoken in me had left me wanting.

It fits you perfect, Brittany replied. *I knew it would.*

What did that mean? *She knew it would?*

Did you see the dress before, Britt? Abby asked before I could.

I stared at the phone, waiting for her response.

Oops, Britt responded. *Typo. I meant to say: It fits you perfect. He knew it would.*

I narrowed my eyes. *Did that even make sense?*

Sorry. Britt was still typing. *That didn't make sense. Fast fingers. I should've said that he must have really known your size. Either way, you look fabulous!*

So strange. But Britt was under a lot of stress lately. Maybe she was starting to crack. I'd have to reach out to her. Maybe we'd need to have a workaholic intervention with her?

There was no time to mention anything else as right then the doorbell rang and my stomach tightened in response.

He's here, I texted the girls. *Gotta go. Talk later.*

I put my phone on silent and rushed to greet my date.

I'd taken Brittany's advice about almost everything when it came to the date with Jessie. Except the car. I'd tried. I really had. But out of the eight cars in my garage, I knew none of them would be appropriate. Jessie still thought I was Dax, a down on his luck salesman of…well, of something I'd never specified. But the point was, the man she knew wasn't wealthy and could hardly show up for a date that he'd already splurged on in a Mercedes, Ferrari, or Aston Martin.

There was no other choice but the bike.

I had no sooner pulled up in front of her small house when the front door opened, and she appeared. Immediately, I hopped off the bike and froze. *Holy shit.* From the moment I met her, I thought Jessie was one of the sexiest women I'd ever seen. Even in that cheap cotton dress, she was curvy and luscious. But damn. Whatever I'd thought before was nothing compared to the way she looked in the dress Brittany had chosen for her.

Cut low in the front, her tits looked amazing with cleavage I would very happily get lost in. The fabric wrapped tight around her waist and tied to the side. The skirt was short enough that as she walked toward me, I caught flashes of her creamy thighs and little glimpses of the garter straps.

It took me a moment to come to my senses. In two steps, I met her on the path and took her hand to help her down the steps. The heels Brittany had sent were *high* and just as I'd predicted, Jessie's legs were perfectly displayed. *More than anything, I wanted them wrapped around my waist while I—*

No.

Later. Tonight was for romance. An actual date. Not just sex. I needed to be a gentleman.

"Sweetheart." Her hand still in mine, I took a step back to appraise her beauty properly. "You look absolutely stunning."

She blushed a little and dipped her head. "Do you like it?"

She truly had no idea how gorgeous she was. I didn't answer. At least not with words. I yanked her toward me. She stumbled a little in her shoes, but I caught her easily and gripped her close with one hand while I took her mouth with mine in a hungry kiss that would leave no doubt about exactly how much I liked the way she looked. *So much for being a gentleman.*

When I was done, I pulled back.

"Dax, thank you for the…" She hesitated. "Well, for everything. The dress, the shoes, and the…"

My eyes traveled to her cleavage.

"You really shouldn't have," she continued.

"You don't like it?"

"No!" Her head shot up. "I love it. I just…I know you said that work was…well, you shouldn't be spending so much money on me is all. You've already been so generous and—"

"Hey." I put a finger to her lips. "It's my pleasure, okay? There is no one I'd rather spoil. So please, don't worry about it. I know what I'm doing."

She looked doubtful, but I waited. Finally, she nodded. "Okay."

"Ready to ride?"

I handed her the helmet before I swung my own leg over the seat. A minute later, I felt the familiar heat of her body pressed up against my back. I reached my hand around and slid it up her thigh until I felt the garter I'd picked out. I couldn't wait to see the full effect. *Later.*

Damn.

I continued traveling my hand up her leg. The flounce of the skirt on the dress protected her from being exposed as we drove, but a smile played at my lips because I knew she would be riding with her bare pussy pressed to the seat. And furthermore, I knew how much she would like it.

I let my finger travel farther up her leg until I felt her shiver. One day apart and we were both hungry for each other.

Still. I needed to show restraint. I pulled my hand away, turned around, and fired up the bike. I tugged my gloves on, and a moment later we sped off into the evening.

"I hope you like sushi." I held my hand out to Jessie and together we walked up the steps into Yama Goya ten minutes later.

"I love sushi."

"You do?" I played stupid and said another silent thank-you to Brittany.

"So much. But it's been ages since I've had anything but diner food."

I squeezed her hand. "Well then, I'm glad I can be the one to treat you to something different. And this place has the best sushi I've had." *And the best little private room*, I thought to myself.

The hostess approached. "Good evening, Mr. —"

"Dax." I cut her off. "Please, call me Dax."

The hostess gave me a strange look. She'd served me many times, and she knew damn well my name wasn't Dax. She also knew how to get a good tip. So, she nodded and smiled. "Of course. Your table is ready for you."

I could feel Jessie's eyes on me, and I realized how close I'd come to blowing it. Maybe I should have told her the truth before I took her out. But no. I hadn't made my billions by second-guessing myself and my decisions, and this was no different. I guided her through the restaurant toward the back, where the hostess opened two sliding screens to reveal a cozy and very private tatami room that consisted of a large slab table set into the floor, and a wide bench covered in thin pillows along the outside.

"Your server will be with you shortly."

I nodded, dismissing the hostess.

Jessie had to sit on the bench and swing her legs over into the tatami in order to get in. It was a good thing there were a number of large potted bamboo plants blocking the entrance to the room from the main dining room. Every man in the place had been watching us as we walked across the floor. I was pretty sure they all would have loved a little glimpse of what was beneath her sexy dress.

And that was not going to happen. This gorgeous creature was all mine.

"This place is beautiful," she said once we were settled, her seated next to me at the large table. "I've never been here. And I've definitely never been in a room like this one."

I grinned. "I like the privacy of this room. You'll see why."

Her eyes widened and her cheeks pinked. With a shaking hand, she reached for her water glass and took a sip. "You must come here a lot. She seemed to know you."

"Once or twice." I shrugged. "I've brought clients here a few times."

"For the sales job you won't tell me about?" Her eyes sparked with challenge.

I liked her fire, but I also didn't want things to get out of hand. I needed to stay in control of the situation.

"You don't need to be in control of this, Jessie. Don't force the answers to questions you think you want the answer to."

Confusion lined her face.

"Just go with it, Jessie. I promise you it's going to be a—"

"I want more!"

A hand flew to my mouth and my eyes widened in surprise. I couldn't believe I'd just blurted that out. I didn't do public scenes or even outbursts of emotion. Ever.

"I'm sorry, Dax. I can't even tell you how much I've enjoyed our time together. It's been—"

"I understand." He pressed his big hand on my bare thigh. The heat from his skin on mine both settled me and fanned the desire that had been building in me since he'd picked me up and kissed me in front of my house. "But you want more."

I nodded. I couldn't help it. As much as I wanted to keep it casual and just sex, Dax was like a drug I couldn't get enough of. Now that I'd had a taste of what it could be like, I needed more and more.

"And I want to give you more."

My heart raced.

His dark eyes seemed to see right through me. "Do you trust me?"

Instantly my mind went back to that first night on the bike. The way I'd let him spank me. Was there any more trust than that? "Completely."

His lips curled up into a smile. "Good." His fingers began stroking my skin, working their way farther up my leg.

I shivered under his touch. I wanted so much more from him. And it wasn't just about this date. It almost scared me how much I'd missed his touch on my skin. The way he looked at me. The way he kissed me.

All of it.

"Have I told you yet how amazing you look tonight?"

I shook my head a little and looked down. It was hard for me to accept compliments. Even from him.

"Hey." He lifted my chin up so I looked him in the eye. "Jessie, you are easily the most gorgeous woman in this building. Hell, in this town. It has taken all of my self-control not to pull you up onto my lap and take you right here and now."

Instantly, heat pooled between my legs, and I shifted in my seat. Dax looked at me so intensely that something inside me clicked, and I believed without even a sliver of doubt that he meant every word.

"You look pretty handsome yourself." He always looked ridiculously sexy. But he'd clearly put a little more effort into his appearance, with a fresh black button-down shirt under his leather vest and dark jeans instead of his usual beat-up denim.

Dax shook off the compliment and focused on me again. His free hand brushed my hair away from my face and over my shoulder. "I wish you could see how sexy you are. You do things to me," Dax continued as his hand slid down to the dip in my dress. His fingers traced the edge of the fabric, teasing the swell of my breasts.

My breath came faster; my tits heaved and strained against the confines of the corset I wore. It was tight. But something about the restriction of the garment added to my building desire.

The hand Dax had on my thigh moved up under my skirt. His fingers toyed with the clip of the garter on my stocking before following the lace up to my sex.

"Dax."

The anticipation of his touch made it hard for me to control my breathing. I wriggled in my seat, unabashedly desperate for him to touch me and see how wet I was. Frustratingly, he wasn't moving further.

"Yes, Jessie?"

My eyes snapped up to him and the wicked grin on his face.

"You're doing it again," he said.

"What am I doing?" My voice pleaded with him.

His fingers slipped under the front of my dress and very casually swept across one nipple, instantly making it impossibly hard against the cup of the corset. A gasp slipped from my mouth and I pushed my chest out and into his hand, wanting more than a simple touch. But the moment I did that, he withdrew it.

"You're trying to control the situation," he said as the finger he had between my legs very briefly flicked over my heat and then it, too, was gone.

I could barely hold myself upright in my seat. My entire body felt like jelly. I ached for a release that not long ago, I hadn't even known existed. But Dax just sat there, studying the drink menu as if he hadn't just ignited an inferno inside me that he wasn't about to extinguish.

I couldn't speak. It took all the effort I had to slow my breathing as the waitress appeared with a discreet knock. I managed a small smile as she presented us with a bottle of sake. Dax confidently placed our order. He looked to me once or twice as he requested a variety of sashimi and rolls. I nodded in agreement, although I was no longer hungry. At least not for rice and fish.

By the time the waitress disappeared and Dax poured us each a glass of the Japanese alcohol, I'd managed to regain my self-control.

"Sorry," I said. "I don't really know what came over me just then."

Dax laughed. "I do."

I raised an eyebrow.

"Sweetheart," he said, his voice full of longing, "you and I are dynamite together. That much we know. But that's not what this night is about."

I swallowed hard.

"You wanted more," he continued. "And so do I. So tonight

is about *more*. I want to know everything there is to know about you." He passed me a glass and we raised them in a toast.

"To us," I said.

"To us," Dax echoed. "Our first date."

We drank deeply. The alcohol warmed my throat.

"Okay," Dax said after he finished his own small cup. "Talk to me." His smile was warm. "Tell me about your kids and Rosie's and how you ended up owning a diner on the edge of town named after another woman."

I laughed and the tension that had been wound up inside me started to unravel as I began talking. Dax genuinely wanted to know all the details about me, and I couldn't remember anyone besides my girlfriends or Stan and Doris ever asking about my kids before. He wasn't scared of the fact that I was a single mom. Quite the opposite, really. He leaned into it, asking more and more questions about them. But I didn't do all the talking either. Dax opened up about his childhood and his days at college. He still didn't want to tell me about his work, but I could respect that not everyone wanted to think about the job while they were having fun. And it didn't seem to matter because the more I learned about Dax, the more I realized it wasn't a part of him that he felt was important to him. There was so much more about him than just his job.

While we talked about all the things, we nibbled on delicious rolls and cuts of sashimi. It had been awhile since I'd handled chopsticks, but Dax patiently helped me. We giggled like teenagers and flirted shamelessly, but just as Dax had promised earlier, the night was about so much more than our sexual connection. We managed to keep our hands off each other despite the privacy the booth would afford us. The buildup of the sexual tension was frustrating, but also fun because I knew how the night would end.

I had just picked up a piece of salmon—after my third attempt with the chopsticks—and was about to put it to my lips when I noticed Dax watching me. He'd put his own chopsticks down and stared at me intently, a small smile on his face.

"What?" I said, suddenly self-conscious. "I know I'm not very good at this, but—"

"You're amazing."

I almost dropped the fish. Somehow I managed to set the bite down before responding. "What?" I tucked a stray strand of hair behind my ear and willed myself not to blush. Dax knew that by now, despite his best efforts to change that.

"You." He reached for my cheek. "Are. Amazing." He spoke every word as he looked me directly in the eyes so I could feel the full impact of them.

A shiver that had nothing to do with our sexual connection traveled through me.

"I don't know why—"

"Jessie." Dax cut me off from what was going to be some sort of excuse as to why I couldn't understand why he might think that. He cupped my cheek and gently stroked a circle with his thumb while he spoke. "You are. Everything about you is absolutely incredible and the more I learn about you, the more I…"

The cool thing to do would be to let that comment go unfinished and not to press the issue. But I was anything but cool and every single feeling that had been growing inside me ever since I'd met my mysterious biker had been building to this very moment.

"The more you what?"

His eyes crinkled in the corners as his handsome smile widened.

"That's easy." His free hand came to cup my other cheek so I couldn't look away as he said, "The more I learn about you, the more I like."

My stomach clenched in what could only be disappointment. But that was silly. *Was I disappointed that he hadn't told me he loved me?* That was ridiculous. We hardly knew each other. Yet, we did know each other. In fact, I felt like I knew Dax in a way that I'd never known any man before. Better even than my ex-husband. We connected on a level I couldn't even begin to explain.

"I *like* you, too." I tried for light and flirty, but I wasn't sure I pulled it off.

"Well, that's a good thing." Dax leaned in and pressed his lips to mine in a soft, sweet kiss. "Because you do things to me, Jessie. I know we haven't been seeing each other for very long, but…"

"I feel it, too."

"Is it crazy?"

"One hundred percent." I nodded. "But I've wasted way too much of my life trying to make sense of things and playing it safe, so I don't care if this is crazy, or moving too fast." I swallowed hard, afraid I'd said too much. But I meant what I said. I wasn't getting any younger and since being with Dax, I'd started to realize how much I'd been missing out on. Never again. "You make me really happy, Dax," I said. "And there can't be anything wrong with that."

"There's absolutely nothing wrong with that," he agreed. "And you make me happy, too," he said. "So very happy."

When he kissed me this time, it was different. Deeper. More meaningful.

God help me, but I was falling for this man.

As the evening went on, we drank more sake until finally my head started to feel a little fuzzy and I switched to water. With every passing moment, I fell a little bit more for my sexy, mysterious biker.

"One more," Dax urged. He used his chopsticks to deftly pick up a spicy tuna roll.

I shook my head. I was so full there was no way I could eat another bite.

"Just one." He dipped the roll into the soy sauce we'd mixed with wasabi and held it out to me.

Never in my life had a man offered to feed me. It seemed all at once to be a seriously sexy move while at the same time being very tender and sweet. I couldn't resist it. No. I couldn't resist *him*.

I leaned forward and took the roll in my mouth, which turned out to be the most delicious piece of the evening.

"Wasn't that good?"

"So good." I dabbed my lips. "All of this was amazing, Dax. Thank you. So much better than the plate of cold fries I'm used to having for dinner."

He chuckled. "Diner food," he said with a shake of his head.

"I know it's not the best but when you spend as much time as I do there, it just makes sense to eat there, too. I've probably spent more time at Rosie's than I have in my house in the last ten years." I hadn't planned to talk so much about the diner. I really didn't want to talk about the takeover or the offer that I still hadn't opened, but we were talking about all the things that were important in our lives and for me, that included Rosie's.

"Why a diner?" Dax asked after the waitress had come to clear our plates. "Have you always been passionate about greasy food?"

I laughed and almost choked on the sip of water I'd taken. "Hardly. It was just a means to an end. When Barrett and I split up, I needed a way to support my kids and be around for them."

"You'd mentioned that." He nodded. "He didn't pay child support?"

"He did." I nodded. "I can say a lot of things about the kind of father Barrett was and wasn't, but he did make his support payments."

"That doesn't make him a good father."

"It certainly doesn't." I really didn't want to talk about my ex-husband. Once the kids turned eighteen, the very little contact I'd had with their father had all but faded away. I preferred it that way. "And that's another reason why I'm so thankful I had the diner," I said. "My employees were like family." I smiled at the memories that flashed through me. "Doris used to help with arts and crafts projects, and Stan is actually a surprising math whiz. While I was cleaning up, they would help the kids with their homework and together, we all...well, we worked."

"What about now?"

The question took me off guard. I sat back in my seat. "Well, Sadie and Lucas are gone to school, so that's all changed of course."

"But the diner? Do you still love it?" There was a question in his eyes that he wasn't asking.

"Love it..."

"I'm sorry if I'm being pushy." Dax reached over and took my hand. "I just see how hard you work and how tired you look. I get the impression that it's been a really long time since you've put Jessica Bateman first."

I nodded, because he was right.

"Maybe Rosie's served a purpose for you and now it's time to move on? Have you ever thought about doing something different?"

More than he knew. It was pretty much all I'd thought about since Trent Thomas had shown up with his offer that I wouldn't be able to refuse.

"I don't know what else I would do." I'd never said that aloud before. "And that's the problem," I said more to myself than to Dax, who watched me carefully. "Without the kids and Rosie's, I don't know who I am."

And that was it. *That* was why I was hesitating on taking the offer. It hit me all at once and made so much sense.

The kids were gone. And now, without the diner, I had no idea who I was or what I would do.

But that didn't matter, because like it or not, I was going to have to figure it out.

Quickly.

"Hey." Dax squeezed my hand and brought me back to the present moment. "I wasn't trying to stress you out."

"I'm not stressed."

He chuckled and reached out to brush a piece of hair from my cheek. "It's all over your face, sweetheart."

I tried for a smile. I didn't want to ruin our perfect date with my personal worries.

"Jessie?"

I nodded.

"You should know that your diner doesn't define you. More than anything, something I've realized is that what you do for a living isn't *who* you are. It's just what you do. And you can always change your mind and do something different. It's never too late. In fact, now that your kids are spreading their wings and doing their own thing, maybe it's the perfect time for you, too?"

I dipped my head and inhaled deeply before looking up. "You're not wrong." He had no idea just how on point he was. And Dax wasn't saying anything that I didn't know in my heart. But hearing it from him somehow made it feel more real and, more importantly, gave me the confidence I needed. "In fact, I think this is the perfect time for so many reasons." I still didn't want to tell him about the takeover. I didn't want to dampen the mood anymore than I already had.

"You mentioned once you liked to paint…"

I almost started to laugh. "I dabbled. A long time ago." I took a deep breath. "Okay. I'm done talking about this." I shook my head so my hair bounced around my shoulders. I flashed Dax what I hoped was a flirty smile, and reached my free hand out to him. I stroked his beard with my hand and gave it a tug. "Distract me."

His eyes flashed with desire and mischief. "Distract you, huh?"

I nodded slowly and bit my bottom lip, ready for part two of our date.

"What kind of distraction?"

"Anything," I said, feeling bold. Dax had already pushed every single one of my boundaries. What was a few more?

He glanced around, his eyes moving slowly around the private booth we were in. Finally his gaze aimed down, to the small space between us that led under the table.

Dax let go of my hand and started to lower himself on the bench.

"What are you—"

"You wanted a distraction." He interrupted me. "So, I'm going to give you one."

"What does that—no!" All at once, I realized what he was going to do. "You can't go under the table and—"

"Why not?" He grinned, his face lined in challenge.

"Because...I..."

"Wouldn't you?" he asked. "Get on your knees under the table for me?"

My eyes widened in shock.

Would I?

Chapter Twelve

SHE WOULD. I knew she would.

Jessie's face blanched when I'd suggested it, but she couldn't fool me. Or herself. The idea of fooling around in public excited her. I could see it in her eyes but I didn't rush her. I let her come to it on her own.

"I would," she said after a moment, just as I knew she would.

My cock thickened in my pants at the thought of Jessie in her sexy dress under the table, on her knees with her sweet mouth wrapped around me.

But better yet would be me returning the favor, driving her to distraction while she tried to act normal, maybe ordering some green tea from the waitress all the while trying not to scream while my tongue was lapping against her clit.

Yes. That would be the perfect dessert.

More than anything, I wanted to push my resolve to be a perfect gentleman on our date aside and do just that, but I held myself in check. Just barely.

"Not tonight, sweetheart."

It wasn't my imagination that I saw disappointment flash

across her face. I could hardly believe that this was the same woman I'd taken for that very first ride on my bike only a few weeks ago. She'd been so timid, so unsure. And now…she got sexier with every second that passed.

"I meant it when I said tonight was about more," I said as a way of explanation. "Don't get me wrong," I continued quickly. "I want to put a pin in this particular discussion because I can't think of any better way to end a nice dinner out."

She grinned and licked her bottom lip, making me groan.

"But not tonight."

It was her turn to groan. "You're killing me."

I chuckled. "The feeling is completely mutual, sweetheart. But I think it's time I took you home now."

The waitress chose that moment to arrive with the check. I didn't even glance at it before pulling my credit card out of my wallet and handing it back to her.

"Dax, let me—"

"No." I cut her off before she could continue. "It's my treat tonight." And it would be my treat for ever after, if I had anything to say about it. She just didn't know that yet. Jessie still thought I was a shitty salesman who wasn't good at his job.

"But it has to be—"

"Jessie." I cut her off, a little more firmly this time. "Please. Let me have this."

The waitress, whom I knew from previous visits to the restaurant, did her best not to smile or let on that she knew exactly who I was and how much money I had. It was a good thing, too. Because her discretion would be earning her a much larger gratuity. I wasn't going to go through all of this for Jessie to find out the truth from anyone else but me. And I'd be telling her later that night. I knew that with certainty, because this date had been so much more than simply a delicious dinner with a beautiful woman.

I couldn't remember ever having such deep conversation with a woman before. I'd told her things I hadn't told anyone. Ever. She was easy to open up to. She seemed to be genuinely interested in everything I had to say. She didn't judge me and, most importantly, she wanted to know more. She wanted to know *me*. Not Shane Grant, the billionaire businessman. But *me*. And that meant more than anything else possibly could.

I finished paying the bill and took Jessie's hand as we moved through the restaurant and out into the cool night air.

"Thank you, Dax." Jessie squeezed my hand. "That was... well, it was..."

I pulled her into me and held her close. "It was the best date I've ever had in my life, Jessie."

It wasn't an exaggeration. My time spent with Jessie—any time—was hands down better than anything I'd ever experienced with a woman before. Ever. It should scare the hell out of me. It should have me running in the opposite direction. After all, I had nothing but bad experience to draw on.

Instead of running, however, I was pulled closer to her.

Even in her high heels, she had to look up into my eyes. "Really?" Her honesty was so refreshing. "But you must have been on so many dates."

She had no idea.

"I've been on a few," I said. "But none of them have ever come even remotely close to being as amazing as this one was." One hundred percent true.

Her smile lit up her face. "It was just dinner."

"It was so much more than *just* dinner. This is ridiculous, but do you believe in fate?"

No doubt I was revealing too much. I should be playing my cards closer to my chest. But I couldn't seem to stop myself.

"Like that we were meant to meet?"

"Exactly." I nodded. "Like I was meant to walk into your diner and see you that night."

"And I was meant to take a chance on a silly pact with my friends and accept your offer?"

There was no way I could keep the grin from my face. "It was meant to be." I held her chin in my hand and kissed her. Our mouths came together softly at first in a gentle kiss to express how I felt about her. But the taste of her on my lips after an entire evening of holding my desire just barely in check was too much. I twined my fingers through her hair and pulled her even closer to me so her breasts were crushed against my chest and deepened the kiss until she moaned into my mouth.

We still stood in the middle of the parking lot. It was dark, only minimally lit, but still we were in plain view of anyone who happened to walk out of the restaurant.

"Dax?"

My name on Jessie's lips was a question that only I had the answer for.

I led her quickly across the parking lot, where my bike was parked next to a large van against the brick wall of the neighboring building.

I shouldn't do this. Hell, I shouldn't even be considering it. I should get on my bike and take her home like a proper gentleman. That was the right thing to do.

But when Jessie turned to me and pressed her body against mine, reaching for my head and pulling it down into a hot kiss full of need, any shred of control I still had snapped. "Fuck," I growled.

"I need you, Dax."

Her words undid me.

In two swift steps, I backed Jessie up against the brick wall. Her hands were on my belt, pulling and pushing the leather through the clasp until it was freed and she could move on to the zipper of my jeans.

While her fingers went to work, I slipped my hand into the

front of her dress and pushed the fabric down to expose the cups of the corset. Her nipples pressed hard against the lacy material I'd picked out for her. I bent and sucked hard on one of her nipples while my fingers rolled the other through the lace. She gasped from my attentions.

And then it was my turn to gasp as she shoved my jeans down and pulled my hard, throbbing cock out and into her hand. She stroked the length of me, squeezing until I thought I might lose my mind if I didn't have her.

Jessie hesitated. "Anyone could see us."

"Yes." I didn't care if the entire world saw us. The only thing I cared about was having her.

"But what if we…"

"Get caught?"

She nodded.

"Is that a problem?" I pushed her dress up over her hips and drank in the sight of her garter, stockings, and bare pussy. I'd really like to have time to properly enjoy that lingerie. But it would have to wait, because at that moment she answered me.

"No," she said. "I need you, Dax. Now."

I did not have to be asked twice.

Thankful once more that we'd abandoned the use of condoms—Jessie had a surgery preventing her from having more children when her twins were born—I lifted her, my hands holding her by her round, juicy ass cheeks so she could lift her legs up and around me. And then I lowered her down on my throbbing cock and filled her completely. She groaned, and I pushed her back hard into the wall. It would have to be fast, but neither of us would need long.

With every thrust, I pumped deeper inside her, and she matched me, squeezing her legs around my back, her sharp heels digging into me. I didn't care.

It didn't take long before I felt her tense around me as her orgasm began to roll through her. A second later, I joined her and together we climaxed hard in mere moments.

I lowered her to the ground and kissed her thoroughly. Tenderly.

There was so much I was feeling in that moment, so much I wanted to say, because I knew without a doubt, for so many reasons, she was the one. Jessie would accept me for who I was, give me the love I never knew I could have, and accept all the love I had to give her. She could be the woman who would be enough for me. She was absolutely everything.

"Jessie..." I cupped her cheek and stroked her soft skin, prepared to tell her everything. But then the door to the restaurant opened and a group of people spilled out, laughing and talking. "We should go," I said instead. I tugged my pants up and into place while she straightened her dress.

It had grown cold while we'd been inside, and the dress she was wearing didn't afford her much cover. I shrugged out of my leather vest and helped her into it before we got on the back of the bike.

"Thank you."

Even in the dim light, I could see that she was thanking me for so much more than simply the warmth of my vest. *Could she be feeling the same way as I was? So quickly?*

Damn, I hoped so.

As we rode through the cool night, Jessie wrapped her arms tight around me and snuggled up tight against my back in a way she never had before. "Tonight was perfect," she said when we pulled up in front of her house. "I wish it didn't have to be over."

I traced my gloved finger over her lip. "It doesn't," I said. "After all, I haven't properly appreciated that lingerie I bought for you."

Her eyes twinkled. "Well, you better come inside then."

146

Dax had never before accepted my invite to come back to my house. But this time, he didn't hesitate to get off his bike and follow me up the walkway. He held my hips and cradled me from behind as I put my key in the lock and opened the door.

We stepped into the small entryway and I'd no sooner turned on a light before Dax spun me around.

"I need to see you, Jessie. Now."

His voice was gruff with need, as if we hadn't just both come incredibly hard up against a brick wall in the middle of a parking lot. But I could understand because I, too, was desperate for him again. My libido was out of control, but Dax brought that out in me. A sex drive I didn't even know was possible.

I didn't hesitate. The irony that it was mere weeks ago when I wouldn't even consider taking off my clothes in front of this man, and now I couldn't wait to strip down, wasn't lost on me.

I shrugged out of his heavy leather vest, letting it fall to the floor before reaching for the simple tie that held my wrap dress closed and tugged. The dress fell open, exposing the sexy lingerie I wore.

I'd spent so much of my life in a simple cotton bra and panties. So much wasted time not knowing how sexy lace and silk could make me feel. Never mind the boning of the corset that pushed me up, nipped me in, and gave my curves definition that would otherwise be impossible. I let the dress fall to the floor and, still in my heels, stepped away from the pile of clothes.

"Damn, woman. Have I told you yet how incredibly sexy you are?"

"Once or twice." Maybe it was the alcohol I'd consumed making me bold, but I didn't think so. It was Dax. It was how much this man desired me that gave me the confidence to step into myself and feel powerful in my sexuality for the first time in my life.

He took a step toward me. His eyes were almost completely dark with desire, his mouth set in a line as if he were only barely keeping himself under control. I knew he'd take me up against the wall or on the floor right there in the entryway. Or even the couch a few feet away. I didn't care. I just wanted him.

His eyes locked on mine as he stalked toward me. "Well, let me tell you again, Jessie." He reached me, and I instinctively backed up against the wall. "You are the most beautiful woman I've ever seen. And the smartest. And the strongest." With every compliment he gave me, his hands moved farther up my sides, tracing the curves the corset created.

I believed him. How could I not? The way he was looking at me left absolutely no room for doubt.

"I want to see you." My hands played with the buttons on his shirt. In all the times we'd been together, Dax had never removed his clothes. More than anything, I wanted to see him and feel him. "Take off your clothes."

His lips twitched up in a sly grin. "Now it's your turn to tell me what to do?"

"When it comes to this? Absolutely." I pushed a button through the hole. And another. "I think it's only fair."

He nodded a little but didn't offer any assistance as I worked my way through his buttons and finally exposed his chest. Greedy, my hands splayed across his hard chest.

Dax closed his eyes and groaned.

Giddy with the small sense of power my touch had over him, I moved my hands up until I could push his shirt over his shoulders, where it, too, fell to the ground.

I let out a shaky breath as I took in the sight of his bare chest. He was strong and defined as I knew he would be, with a sprinkle of chest hair I tangled my fingers through as I explored him. But there was still so much to discover.

Next, I worked my hands over his belt and button of his jeans. I bent my knees, and pushed his pants down to where he could step from them as well. He kicked his boots off and then he was completely naked, towering over me where I still crouched in front of him. I'd seen it before of course, but with Dax completely naked, his hard cock looked that much more impressive. Slowly, I trailed my hands up his thighs and moved to my knees. I gripped his length in both hands and dipped my head to take him in my mouth.

He moaned and his hands threaded through my hair.

I had no idea what I was doing. I'd only ever given head once before. Or I should say, I tried. Barrett didn't believe in oral sex. Not that I was thinking about my ex-husband at all with my mouth around my new lover. Not. At. All.

Dax was clearly enjoying my attentions as I licked and sucked. My own sense of power and sexuality grew with every moan that slipped from my rough and gruff biker man.

"Jessie." He spoke my name on a growl but I didn't stop. "Jessie," he said again, more forcefully and then before I could even contemplate stopping, he bent and lifted me up to my feet. His breath came fast as he pressed me up against the wall. "Damn, woman. I didn't think it was possible to want you more than I do at this moment."

The feeling was more than mutual. I tipped my head, and his lips pressed to mine in a hungry kiss.

I let my hands trail down his naked back, digging into his firm buttocks, urging him on. "Dax, I need—"

"No." He growled. "Not like this."

Before I could protest—and dammit, I *was* going to protest —Dax took one step back and lifted me as if I weighed nothing.

"What are you doing?" He'd flipped me over his shoulder

so my head hung down, affording me a very nice view of his ass. But I couldn't enjoy it because he had no business lifting me like that. He was going to hurt himself. "Dax, I'm too heavy. Put me—"

"Jessie."

I squirmed and his hand clamped down on my ass, holding me in place.

"You are not heavy. And if I don't get you out of this hallway soon, I'm going to regret it. Which one is your bedroom?"

He didn't wait for an answer. As if I was in fact not heavy, Dax strode down the short hallway, directly to the open door—my room—and deposited me on the bed.

I landed on the comforter with a soft plop, my legs spread, my knees bent, and my hair fanned out behind me.

"There," Dax said with a satisfied grin. "Much better."

There was truly nothing hotter than the sight of Jessie sprawled on her bed in front of me, wearing the lingerie I'd picked out just for her. Except for maybe the sight of her on her knees in front of me with my cock in her pretty mouth. That was hot as fuck.

But this...

The last woman I'd taken to bed was my ex. Since then, I'd very purposely avoided the bedroom, keeping all of my sexual conquests as far away as possible. There was an intimacy in a bedroom, and that was the last thing I wanted when I was with a woman.

Until now.

Until Jessie.

Jessie, I *needed* in the bedroom. I needed all of her. I knew that now with complete conviction.

She propped herself up on her elbows and her long, dark hair fell over her shoulder. I could have watched her for hours, just taking in the gift that was the sight of her dressed in black lace and silk. But when she tilted her head with a smile and said, "It would be so much better if you were down here with me," I couldn't help but agree. That *would* be better.

I crawled over her onto the bed, taking my time as I traveled up her body. Her skin was smooth and soft and smelled vaguely of vanilla and cinnamon. A sweet and spicy combination, just like her. She moaned impatiently as I kissed each of her thighs in turn, worshipping every inch of her before finally slowly moving between her legs.

Jessie sucked in a breath and arched her back as I licked her seam before dipping inside her wet heat. It didn't take long before she squirmed beneath me, but I didn't want her to come that way. I wasn't even close to being finished with her.

"Dax," she pleaded but I left her wanting and once more resumed my expedition up her gorgeous curvy body, still wrapped in the beautiful present of the corset.

"Not yet, sweetheart."

Her chest heaved and strained against the confines of the lingerie. I could hardly believe her tits were contained by the scraps of fabric at all. Easily, I pulled the material down to free each of her breasts so I could properly knead, suck, and tweak them. Jessie's hands clenched the comforter beneath her, and I knew she was getting close. But still, I wasn't done. I wanted to enjoy every second of her—of us—in her bed for the first time.

"Dax." She groaned. "I need you." Her hips thrust up toward me.

I kissed her. One hand twined through her hair, the other bracing me against the mattress as I used my knee to nudge her legs farther apart. My mouth still on hers, I pressed achingly slowly into her heat.

Jessie groaned into my mouth as I entered her.

I lifted my lips from hers so I could look in her eyes as I held my body still. When our eyes locked, I started to move. Slowly, so slowly, so we could feel every inch of each other as we came together.

We stayed that way for a few moments, staring into each other's eyes as we moved together, making love. Our connection was so intense, the only thing that could bring me to break it was the need to have her mouth on mine again.

Jessie's hands gripped my back as if she were afraid I might leave. But I wasn't going anywhere. Not ever. This woman was home. She was everything.

When I felt the familiar tremble of her body beneath me, my own groin tightened with imminent release. I reluctantly pulled away from her sweet lips, because I needed to look in her eyes as we came together.

Moments later, our moans filled the air as we hit our climaxes at the same time. They crashed through us. Powerful wave after wave until, finally spent, I kissed her again.

It was the single most intense moment of my entire life. I had no idea it could be this way. That any woman could make me feel this way.

Reluctantly, I lowered myself from her and moved onto my side, where I could pull her against me. I held her tightly, running my fingers through her hair, and pressing kisses to the back of her neck.

"Dax, that was…"

"I know." I nestled her closer to me. "Sweetheart, I know," I murmured in her ear. "Fucking amazing."

She nodded a little, her head growing heavy.

"You," I continued, "are fucking amazing." They weren't adequate words to describe how she really made me feel. I didn't have the slightest idea how to explain to Jessie how I felt about her. I'd never made love to a woman before. Not like that. Not even my ex. Not even close. The connection between us had been the single most intense thing I'd ever experienced, and there was only one explanation for it.

"Jessie?"

"Mmm," she murmured.

I knew she was close to sleep.

I nuzzled my face in her hair and filled my senses with her before finally whispering, "I love you."

Chapter Thirteen

I WOKE to the distant sound of a motorcycle, as if it were in my dream. But when I opened my eyes and the space next to me in the bed was empty, I knew it wasn't a dream. *Dax was gone.*

The alarm clock across the room told me it was just after seven.

He'd stayed the night.

My lips curled into a smile.

I'd slept deeply after we'd made love. *Made love?* Yes. It was the only way to describe what had transpired between us in my bed. It was the most amazing sexual experience I'd ever had and that was saying something, considering everything I'd experienced with Dax in the last few weeks. But it had been more than just sex. So much more. And when we were done, I was so completely physically and mentally exhausted, I wasn't sure I'd be able to move my body.

Not that I had to. Dax wrapped me in his arms and held me tight. The last thing I remembered before I'd drifted off only moments later was feeling safe, protected, and…*loved.*

Dax had told me he loved me. *Didn't he?*

I sat up in bed, the quilt falling away to reveal the lingerie I'd slept in.

Had I dreamt it? Had he really said *I love you?*

There was a note on the pillow next to me that answered the question for me.

Sweetheart,

You were sleeping so peacefully I didn't want to wake you but I had to get to work. Last night was amazing.

P.S. You weren't dreaming.

I smiled and clutched the note to my chest.

He loved me.

And it felt absolutely amazing, because I had never in my life felt the way I did about Dax. Even with Barrett, the feelings didn't even come close. It could only be love the way my body thrilled at the thought of him. The way he looked at me. Touched me. And listened to me. Our date had been the best night of my life. And it wasn't just the sex—although that was mind-blowing—but the way Dax had listened to me talk about everything that was important to me. And not only had he been interested, but he also really seemed to care.

And when it came to Rosie's, maybe he was right. Maybe it *was* time for me to try something different. Maybe even follow my dreams. Or figure out what my dreams were. Either way, for the first time since the developers had started coming around, I actually felt good about accepting the offer and—

The offer.

I'd forgotten all about it. Not that it mattered. Not really. My mind was made up. I was going to take it, no matter what it was. Not only was I out of time and options, but I was ready. Abby had promised to put me in touch with a lawyer who would make sure I was getting the best deal possible, but I didn't need it. It didn't matter. The sooner I took the offer, the better. I was ready to move on. And now I knew that whatever my future looked like, it would include Dax.

Before I could manage to muster the energy to pull myself out of bed, I reached for my phone and pressed the button that would call Sadie. I promised my daughter I'd check in after my night out. Besides, now that I knew with certainty that I planned to continue to see Dax, I wanted my kids to know about him, too.

"Mom," she answered on the second ring. "How was your night out? You were pretty cagey about what you were doing," she teased.

I'd always had an easy relationship with my kids. It came naturally, because it had always been the three of us.

"That's why I'm calling, actually," I said. "Sadie, I want to tell you something. I actually really want to tell you both something. Do you think we should get Lucas on the call?"

Sadie laughed. "Are you kidding? Lucas doesn't have classes today. He'll be sleeping until well after lunch time, if I know my brother."

And she did know him. Better than anyone.

"Maybe it should wait then," I said. "I kind of wanted to—"

"No way!" Sadie cut me off. "It's not my fault he's lazy. Tell me, Mom." She laughed. "Wait, let me guess."

I shook my head, amazed as always at my daughter's never-ending energy. "Go ahead."

"You're dating someone."

My mouth fell open. "How…what…why would you…"

"I was right!" She laughed again. "I knew it. You've been so *busy* lately," Sadie continued. "I mean, you're always busy but this felt different."

"What do you think about that?" I was nervous to ask. After all, the kids had never known me to date at all. *Would they be okay with it? What if they weren't? What would I do?*

"I think it's great, Mom. Really." She didn't even hesitate to tell me. "And Lucas will be thrilled, too. Although, fair warning," she continued. "He'll probably try to be all protective or something. But honestly, Mom. We're happy for you. You've spent way too much time alone. You deserve this."

My head spun with the maturity of my daughter. Then again, deep down I'd known they'd be pleased. They were great kids.

"That makes me happier than I can even tell you," I said. "And I really want you to meet him next time you come to visit, okay?"

We talked for another few minutes. I told Sadie the basics about Dax before we changed topics and she filled me in on everything going on in her world. We made plans to have a video chat with all three of us soon before we disconnected the call.

I stripped out of the lingerie and stretched my arms over my head, allowing myself to feel the delicious soreness that was starting to be familiar as the aftereffects of a night of passion with Dax. It had become a constant state of being lately and I loved it.

I wrapped my robe around my body and padded into the kitchen, stepping over my clothes and Dax's vest that I'd been wearing the night before where they still lay in the hallway. My lips curved up into a smile at the memory of what we'd done in the hallway up against the wall before even making it to the bedroom.

I put a pot of coffee on and only then did I take the envelope Trent Thomas had given me the day before out of my purse. The last offer had been less than a year's income for me. On a good year. Which it wasn't. So, truthfully, the first offer that had been presented would be equivalent to what I would bring home that year. If I was lucky.

The new number written on the paper was larger. By about twenty thousand. It still wasn't much money. And maybe a few days ago, I would have balked at it. But now? I sighed and picked up my cell phone. I texted Trent Thomas at the number on the paper.

I'm coming in this morning. I'll take the offer.

His reply came quickly.

Glad to hear it. See you soon.

Walking away from Jessie, who somehow looked at once both sweet and sinfully sexy fast asleep in her bed earlier, had been the hardest thing I'd done in recent memory. There was nothing more that I wanted to do than climb back under the covers and wake her up by kissing every inch of her before telling her over and over that I loved her.

It was corny as hell, but I felt like I was walking on air as I finally pushed through the doors of my office after running home for a quick shower and change. As much as I would have loved to ignore work, only days after the acquisition was final, I knew there'd be a few things to take care of. With any luck, I could finish up quickly, clear my desk of anything important, and get back to my love.

She'd been drifting off to sleep the night before after our lovemaking, so I couldn't be sure that she'd heard me tell her that I loved her.

But it didn't matter, because I'd tell her again and again and again.

Just thinking about that moment made me grin so wide that I got more than one strange look as I walked through the lobby of my offices, greeting my employees. It had been a long time since I'd shown up at the offices feeling so light, and it had very little to do with the merger being wrapped up. There was no stress relief better than being in love. I knew that now.

It was Jessie.

She made me happy in a way I didn't know was even possible. Hell, Jessie made me want things I never thought I'd want. Like a family. Maybe not children of my own, but…the way she spoke of her children with so much pride and love the night before, it had made me think and much to my surprise, the idea of it all just felt right.

But I was rushing myself. I laughed aloud at my eagerness.

"Mr. Grant?" Kenny stood next to me—my cup of coffee in his hand, a look of bewilderment on his face. "Are you okay?"

"No," I answered seriously and took my coffee with a nod of thanks. "I'm not okay at all, Kenny."

My assistant's eyes opened wide as he went into damage control mode. No doubt the eager young man had already started making mental lists of how he could assess and mitigate whatever situation it was that was making things not okay. I chuckled and grabbed his shoulder with a gentle squeeze. "I'm absolutely fantastic," I clarified before the man exploded. "Nothing to worry about here, Kenny."

I moved through the lobby toward my office and once

recovered, Kenny quickly caught up. "I'm glad to hear it, Mr. Grant. It's been a long road with the merger, and I know how stressed you've been. It's been a lot of pressure and—"

"That's all behind us now, Kenny." I walked through the door he opened before I could get there and into my office. The young man really did need a raise. I hadn't noticed all the little details of the things he did to make my life run smoothly. Everything was clearer now. As if being in love had lifted the fog I'd been living my whole life in.

"You should take a day off, Kenny."

"Pardon me, Mr. Grant?" He did a double take and looked up from where he was straightening a stack of papers on the edge of my desk. "The day—"

"Off." I grinned. "You deserve it. Why don't you take the rest of the day off?"

Suspicion flickered in his eyes. "But I have to—"

"It can wait." I clapped my hands together. "What needs to be done today? The merger is complete. We're in the clear. I'm sure I can manage for a few hours without you."

Kenny looked doubtful, which was fair. But it was one day, no big deal.

"I'm serious, Kenny." I walked around my desk so I could put my arm over his shoulders. I guided him through my office and to the door. "Enjoy yourself."

"Are you sure, Mr. Grant?"

I knew if I said the word, he'd turn right around, but I meant what I said. Kenny worked hard. He deserved a break. And a raise. But one thing at a time. "I'm sure. Go," I said. "Before I change my mind."

He hesitated, but only for one more moment. I leaned against my doorjamb and watched while he grabbed his things and left for the day. It was a little thing, but it made me feel good. Never mind that I really didn't know what was needed of me or whether I had any meetings I shouldn't miss. Not that it mattered. I was confident I could figure it out. After all, I used to get by without an assistant. I laughed again, garnering even more looks from my employees, who were trying not to stare.

They'd never seen me looking so relaxed. So...happy.

Well, that was about to change. Because now that Jessie was in my life, just thinking about her smile and her laugh, the sound of her—

Voice?

But that was impossible. I'd left Jessie at home, in bed. She didn't even know where my office was, let alone *who* I was. A little fact I planned to remedy later that day. But why would Jessie be here, in my office?

And then I heard Trent. The voices were still out of sight, around the corner from where I stood.

"Thank you for coming in so quickly."

"Honestly, I'm glad I did," Jessie said. "Once I made up my mind, I just wanted to sign and be done with it all."

My brain couldn't keep up with what was happening, or why she was there in my offices, talking to Trent. But then it didn't matter because before I even thought to move, Trent and Jessie rounded the corner together and stopped. Directly in front of me.

My heart stuttered the way it always did when I saw Jessie. She was so beautiful. I stepped toward her. A reflex. "Jessie."

"Dax?" Jessie's face twisted in question. "I didn't know you worked—"

"What are you doing here?" I moved to take her hand. It took a great effort not to pull her into my arms and kiss her.

But her face was still lined with questions.

"Dax?"

I heard the confusion in Trent's voice, but I only had eyes for my love.

"I didn't realize the two of you knew each other, Shane."

Jessie's eyes flashed, and I saw the exact moment she realized who I was. Her pupils dilated. She dropped my hand. "Shane?" She took a step back and looked to Trent before locking eyes with me once more. "Why did he call you Shane?"

She already knew the answer. I could see it in her eyes. All of the dots were connected. Pieces I didn't even realize were missing—put together. It made sense.

I reached for her hand again but she took another step back.

"Why," she asked again, slower this time, "did he call you Shane?"

"Jessie, I can—"

"You two know each other?"

I'd almost forgotten that Trent was still standing there.

"How do you—"

"No." Jessie's voice was cold and controlled. "I don't think we know each other at all." She tilted her head, her eyes narrow. "Shane, is it? Shane *Grant*?"

I swallowed hard at the emphasis on my last name.

She nodded slowly and took a deep breath in what was clearly an effort to compose herself. I still didn't know why she was there, but it didn't matter. All that mattered was that this wasn't how she was supposed to learn the truth. I was going to tell her my way. In private. In a way she'd understand and... not like this.

"It makes sense now." She chuckled but there was absolutely no humor in it. "I'm such an idiot."

"Jessie. I—"

"No." She cut me off with a sharp shake of her head. "I see how it is. You played me, and I totally fell for it."

What?

"I mean," she continued with a sharp laugh, "I knew it was pretty unbelievable that a man like you could be into..." She inhaled and shook her head, unable to say what she was thinking. "Wow.. I can't believe how stupid I am. But I guess the joke's on me. It worked." She looked directly at me. "You actually made me believe it was possible to follow my dreams."

That harsh laugh again. The sound killed something inside me.

"But it's over now." Jessie nodded her head toward Trent. "I signed the offer. You win."

The offer? Signed?

Trent.

It all clicked at once. Why Jessie was with Trent. The offer she signed.

Fuck.

"Jessie," I tried. "No, it's—"

"Fuck you." She spat the words and pain twisted her face. "Fuck. You."

Chapter Fourteen

I'D LEFT Dax's car, his stupid gift, in the parking lot of his offices. *How could I have been so stupid?* He gave me a car, and I still couldn't see it. What kind of man gave a complete stranger a *car*? A billionaire, that's who. A billionaire with a diabolical plan.

And it worked.

He'd succeeded.

It was probably a good thing I wasn't driving. I was so furious I couldn't see straight, never mind the tears that were burning behind my eyelids, waiting to spill down my cheeks. If I wasn't so angry, I might actually cry. But I wouldn't. No. Especially not in the back of my rideshare. I couldn't. Not with the driver watching me in the rearview mirror as if I might snap at any moment into some kind of murderous rage.

And I might, too.

If I wasn't so completely destroyed.

Shit.

So much for no crying in front of a stranger.

I swiped at my tears and shifted my body so I stared out the window. That was twice in only a few weeks that I'd cried.

And I never cried. Of course, I'd never had my life twisted upside down *and* had my heart ripped out in such a short time.

"Are you okay back there?" The driver's voice reached me as I blew my nose.

I really did need to get my own car.

I guess I'll have the money to finally get one. The laugh that erupted from my throat was anything but humorous.

"Are you okay, ma'am?" the driver asked again, his voice trepidatious and in no way prepared for the truth.

"I'm fine," I lied, to his obvious relief.

I was *not* fine. I didn't think I'd ever be fine again. In the span of ten minutes, I'd lost my diner, my livelihood, and my dignity. Never mind my broken heart. But that was my own fault. I'd let myself be fooled.

How could I have been so stupid? How could I not have seen that Dax—or *Shane* or whatever his name was—had only been playing me to help his buddy? Rich, powerful men screwing over the small business owner—literally—just because they could.

The worst part was, if I closed my eyes, I could still feel his hands on me. His kisses on my lips. The way he moved inside me while his eyes were locked with mine.

Damn. He was a good actor. And I'd fallen for his act one hundred percent. He'd made me believe that this overweight, overworked, frumpy, sexually inexperienced, mother of two with the stretch marks to prove it, could possibly be sexy and desirable. That I could ever attract a sexy biker sex god who would worship and accept all of me.

I believed him when he told me I was sexy.

I believed him when he said he couldn't get enough of me.

That I was special.

That there was no reason I couldn't follow my dreams.

That he *loved* me.

I swallowed a sob as it slipped from my throat. My hand clasped over my mouth as if I could forcibly contain my pain.

The driver's eyes flicked back to me in the mirror and quickly to the road as we pulled into the parking lot of Rosie's.

I muttered a quick thank-you and slipped from the car before he could ask me whether I was okay again. I didn't think I could keep lying, and I was about to face much harder questions in a few moments when Doris and Stan found out that they were both going to be out of jobs.

Because it wasn't just me that I had to think about.

I stood and stared at the diner I had called home for ten years. Rosie's had represented my freedom from my ex-husband. It was so much more than strong coffee, pieces of pie, and plates of fries. It was financial independence and being there for my children. It was where Lucas and Sadie had grown up. Where I'd heard about their day at school, where more than once I wiped tears after a bad day. The very parking lot where I stood was where I'd taught each of my children how to drive. Round and round. Stop. Start. Stop. Start.

"Stop it, Jessie." I spoke aloud, straightened my shoulders, and tossed my hair back.

Fundamentally, I knew that taking the offer was the only option I had. It was time for me to move on.

The familiar bells over the door tinkled as I walked inside the empty diner. Doris and Stan both looked up from their stools at the counter. They were playing cards during working hours, and I couldn't even be mad. There were no customers and without even asking, I knew there'd been none all morning.

I took a deep breath.

"Jessie?" Stan jumped up from his seat. "Are you okay? You look—"

"Terrible," Doris chimed in with her usual no-nonsense approach. "Let me get you a coffee."

I nodded. "Thank you. I'm fine. I just…no. I'm not fine." Both my employees stopped and stared at me. I'd always tried my best to stay positive when it came to Rosie's. Especially lately. "I need to tell you both something. Please sit."

They both listened and nodded as I told them the abbreviated story of Trent Thomas and his development company. I left out the personal details. They weren't important. "I'm sure you both saw this coming," I said as I finished up. It really wasn't a long story. "We barely have any customers at all anymore."

Stan stood and gave me a hug. "I'm sorry, kiddo."

Hot tears threatened again. "I should be the one who's sorry." I sniffed loudly. "You'll both need new jobs and I—"

Doris burst out in a loud, throaty laugh. "She's so cute, isn't she, Stan?"

Stan grinned. "She sure is."

"What are you two talking about?" I looked between them.

Doris stood and took Stan's hand. "We've been ready to retire for years, Jessie."

I couldn't look away from their joined hands. "Are you… you're…"

"We've been together for what?" Doris looked to Stan. "Six years now?"

My mouth fell open. "How did I not know?"

"You had a few things to think about," Stan said. "And two beautiful kids to raise. Truth is, Jessie, Doris and I were waiting until you were ready. We weren't going to leave you before the kids graduated."

"And now…"

"Seems like a good time for all of us to try something new, don't you think?"

I nodded and pulled them in for a hug. I had no idea they both cared so much about me and my kids. They'd stayed for me. It was like salve to my aching heart to know how much they'd cared all these years.

After a bit more hugging and a few more tears—mostly from me, but also a few from Stan—I sent them both home. There was no point staying open anymore.

I watched them drive away before I flipped the sign to Closed and drew the blinds shut for the last time.

After Jessie left, it took me a few minutes to process what had just happened and what she *thought* had happened. All around me, my employees scattered and tried to pretend that they hadn't just been witness to the biggest dramatic scene our office had ever seen.

I turned to Trent, who still stood next to me. "Let me see it," I demanded, just barely keeping my voice in check.

"See what?"

"The offer." I spoke through clenched teeth. "In my office." There was no point in giving anyone anything else to gossip about.

I didn't wait for his reply before I retreated to my office and dropped into my chair behind my desk.

My friend was right behind me. He put the papers flat on the wood in front of me and slid it toward me.

"You know this is confidential."

"Fuck confidential."

I snatched up the papers and it was just as I thought. An offer to acquire Jessie's diner, or more specifically, the land it sat on. *I should have known.* How could I have *not* known? It's not as if I was a frequent patron of Rosie's or of the area where the diner sat. Was that why I hadn't noticed that the land was prime for acquisition and development? Even in weeks of visiting Jessie at the diner, I'd noticed how the area had grown quieter and quieter as more businesses shut down.

Maybe I just hadn't wanted to see it.

I flipped quickly through the papers Trent had placed in front of me. A simple contract for acquiring her land for what should have been an illegally small sum of money. And there it was, Jessie's signature. She'd signed it away. Her diner. Her livelihood. Her *home*. It was so much more than just some greasy spoon at the edge of town. She'd told me as much and I'd seen it in her eyes. Rosie's had been her home. Where she'd raised her children and gained her independence.

I shook my head as I went through the contract again.

"It's all legit," Trent said. "Pretty standard."

My head shot up and my eyes narrowed on my friend. "Legit? Maybe. But this is a bullshit offer and you know it." My rage simmered just under the surface. Barely contained. Jessie had just lost everything, and it was my friend who'd taken it from her. Dammit. I'd *helped* him. I'd given him an office to work out of. And worse, just the night before, I'd encouraged Jessie to try something new. To follow her dreams and think about leaving the diner behind.

I didn't know.

But she did.

And she'd trusted me and my advice.

Would she have signed if I hadn't been so encouraging?

There was no way to know. But what I did know was that I had, at least in some small way, contributed to this.

The look of betrayal and pain on her face filled my mind. It was easy to see why she might think I was involved. Hell, the evidence was pretty damning.

"It's not bullshit, Shane," Trent said. "It's standard. I already raised my offer once."

I dropped the papers on the desk in front of me. "And you're telling me you wouldn't have gone higher?" I wasn't a fool, and Trent knew it. "You needed her land. I *know* you would have gone higher than this, Trent. A lot higher."

He shrugged. "It's business, Shane. It's not personal."

"That's where you're wrong, Trent. It is *very* personal."

He must have seen something in my eyes, because wisely my friend chose that moment to retrieve the papers and back out of my office.

I waited until he shut the door behind him before picking up my water glass and hurling it at the door.

"Fuck!"

Logically, I knew that it wasn't Trent's fault. He was right. It was just business. Anyone else, and he would have done the same thing. It was all about the bottom line. And it's not as if the buyout was a small amount of money. Still, it would hardly be enough to get Jessie's kids through school and buy her a new car. Never mind her mortgage payments on her tiny house or any traveling she might want to do. And if she did decide to follow her dreams and paint, she'd need start-up money and maybe some training. It wasn't enough money. It wasn't even close.

I couldn't just sit there and do nothing. I pushed up from my desk so hard that my chair crashed into the wall behind it and clattered to the floor but I didn't care.

A knock sounded at my door.

I spun and growled, "Go away."

The door opened.

Whomever it was clearly didn't value their job. Or their life.

"Shane?" Brittany Donahue walked through the door and quickly shut it behind her.

I shook my head and turned away from her.

"Are you going to tell me what happened earlier?" she asked. "I got in late this morning and the office is buzzing.

Something about a curvy brunette woman who told you off in front of everyone."

There was a flicker of humor to her voice, which meant she couldn't possibly know the extent of what had happened, because I doubted very much that she would find anything funny about the truth.

"Did Jessie find out who you are and give you hell?"

I turned and nodded.

"Shit." The smile fell from Brittany's face. "I was kidding, Shane. I didn't...what happened?"

"You really didn't hear?"

Brittany stepped farther in the office and without waiting for an invitation, sat in the chair across from my desk. "I'm not going to lie, people are talking, but I make it a policy not to listen to office gossip, so no, I didn't hear all the gory details. I was teasing a minute ago. I—"

"It's fine." I shook my head. "No. It's not fine. But...I assume you're going to find out sooner or later anyway." I sank down in the chair across from her and dropped my arms on the desk. "Maybe you knew that Jessie's diner was the subject of an acquisition?"

She nodded. "I did hear something about that. Abby said Phillip was going to get her a lawyer."

"Well, I don't think that happened. Or if it did, that lawyer should be fired. She signed Rosie's away this morning."

"She did what?"

It was the first time I'd ever seen my CFO look distraught.

"She wouldn't have done that. I mean, not without legal advice. Why would she—"

"I encouraged her to do it."

Brittany's pretty face twisted into a snarl. "You did what?"

I held up my hands in defense. "It wasn't like that. I didn't know. I swear. She didn't tell me about the acquisition. I didn't know anything about it. I promise." I needed Brittany to believe me. It wasn't much, but it was a start and maybe if she believed me, Jessie might, too. "I would have advised her to get a lawyer. I never would have suggested she just sign it away at the first shitty offer she got." I dropped my head in my hands. "But she thinks that I did know. She thinks I was in on it and that everything between us was fake." I rubbed at my temple and finally looked up to see Brittany watching me.

She didn't say anything for a moment, but finally she asked, "But it wasn't, was it? Fake, I mean." Her stare bored holes in me. "You care about her."

It wasn't a question, but I nodded anyway. "Brittany, I'm in love with her." She opened her mouth, but before she could protest, I quickly added, "I know it's early and things have moved really fast. But I swear to you, Brittany. I have never felt this way about anyone in my whole life. Jessie is special. She's amazing and sexy and strong and…"

I couldn't finish the sentence. Emotion choked my throat. I dropped my head down again, unable to focus on Brittany or anything else except what I'd screwed up.

After a moment, I heard Brittany stand.

"I believe you," she said when I looked up. "But the thing is, it doesn't matter what I believe."

I jumped to my feet. I wanted to ask her what to do. I wanted to call Kenny back from his day off and have him help me. I wanted to manage my way out of the situation, but I knew I couldn't.

"I'm going to take the rest of the day off," Brittany said when she reached the door.

I nodded. Jessie needed her. It was understood. Jessie needed her friends to help her through this massive life event. Not me. What she didn't need was me—the man she thought betrayed her trust and broke her heart.

I'm not sure how long I sat in the empty booth, picking at the spot where the Formica was chipping on the table, before I heard the familiar bells over the door tinkle. My head shot up and I twisted around to see who it was. But I already knew who it was. Abby had a spare key.

Besides, I knew they would come.

"There she is!"

"Jessie!"

"I'll put some coffee on."

The diner filled with my friend's voices, their energy injecting some life into the room. And then Sandy was sliding into the booth next to me, pulling me into a tight hug. "I got you," she whispered into my ear as she held me tight. For such a petite woman, her grip was insanely strong. A fact I was thankful for as I melted into her embrace and let myself cry.

"I don't cry," I managed to mutter into her shoulder between sobs.

"Yes. You do," she said calmly. "And it's okay. Cry. It's good for you."

To Sandy's credit, she didn't let up on her hold while I sobbed into her shoulder despite the fact that my tears soaked through her sweater. She murmured comforting words into my ear and rubbed circles on my back until finally, I had no more tears to cry. It was only then that she pulled back and, with a tissue that had appeared out of nowhere, dabbed at my cheeks as if I were one of her little girls.

"Did you get it all out?"

I nodded. And then promptly shook my head with a small laugh.

"Yeah," Sandy said. "I don't think so either. But for now, maybe a cup of coffee and some friend time will help."

I nodded and turned to see that Abby and Darla had joined us in the booth. Abby slid the cup of coffee in front of me. I wrapped my hands around it and stared down into the dark liquid.

"Thank you for coming. How did you know?"

"I called them."

My head shot up to see Brittany standing next to the table, just a little bit back, as if she were unsure.

I let my eyes meet hers and for the first time, I made the connection I'd been trying to ignore.

She knew.

She. Knew.

Of course she knew. She worked for Shane Grant. She'd seen him that night. That first night I went with him on his bike. She knew when I called him Dax that it wasn't his name. That the dress would fit. Trent Thomas was working out of her offices. She knew. *Had she been in on it, too?*

My heart squeezed. I didn't think I could handle it if my best friend had betrayed me. It was one thing to learn that the man you thought you were falling in love with was a traitor. But for it to be your best friend too?

No.

I shook my head and narrowed my eyes in her direction. "Get out," I said through clenched teeth.

It was only when Sandy put her hand over mine that I realized it was in a tight fist.

"Jessie." Brittany took a step closer. "I didn't know. I swear."

"Liar." I spoke the word simply. As the fact it was.

"No," Brittany said. "I'm not—"

"Get. Out!" I shoved against Sandy until I stood in front of Brittany. Vaguely I registered her red eyes, her lack of makeup, and her messy hair. Brittany never looked anything less than perfect. But I didn't care. "Get out of my diner!" I pointed a shaking hand at the door and took a step toward her. "It's still mine," I said. "At least for the time being. And I don't want

you anywhere near it. Or me." She took one small step backward, but still, I came to stand in front of her, only inches
away.

"Jessie…"

"I can't believe you did this to me." The surge of anger I'd
felt was dissipating, leaving me sad. Very, very sad. "You…Brit-
tany…" I dropped my head as more tears flooded my eyes. For
a woman who'd hardly cried in the last twenty years, I was sure
making up for it now.

"Jessie," Brittany said again. "I'm sorry I didn't tell you
who Dax really was."

I listened, but I didn't look up.

"Yes, it's true that I knew who he was that night. And
honestly," she continued, "it's the only reason I agreed to the
stupid pact. Do you really think I could let you go off with a
stranger in the night?"

Behind me, I heard Abby protest, but I still didn't look up
as Brittany continued.

"I knew it would be okay, because despite his reputation
with women, Shane Grant is a good guy."

My head shot up then. "Good guy?"

She was already shaking her head. "I know you think that
he did this to you on purpose, but Jessie…I just don't know if I
believe that. He's not that kind of guy. He didn't know."

I squeezed my eyes shut against her words.

"And Jessie? *I* didn't know. I swear to you on my life, Jessie.
I didn't know anything about the acquisition until Abby
mentioned it to me the other day. I've been working so hard
with this merger that I honestly didn't even pay attention to the
new guy in the office. I haven't even *met* Trent Thomas yet."

I wanted to believe her.

"I don't know exactly what went down with Shane, and I
wasn't there this morning, but I *can* tell you that by the time I
got to the offices, all hell had broken loose. He's out for blood.

I've worked with him for a while now, Jessie. And I can honestly say I've never seen him this upset."

We'd been friends for a long time. A *very* long time. We'd been through it all together. The worst and the best. There were very few people I knew as well as I knew Brittany, and they all stood behind me, letting the scene play out. Letting us figure it out.

Her eyes shone with unshed tears and they pleaded with me to believe her. My head hurt from everything that had happened and everything she'd just said. I didn't know what to think when it came to Dax or Shane or whoever the hell he was. But I knew my best friend.

"I believe you." The words were barely a whisper but it didn't matter because a second later, I was wrapped in her arms and we were both crying.

"I swear, Jessie. I'd never do anything I thought would hurt you. Ever."

"I know."

And I did. Even through the pain, I knew in my heart that none of my girlfriends would ever hurt me. Not intentionally.

When we were done hugging—and crying—Darla guided us back to the booth.

"What did you mean when you said he has a reputation with women?" I asked Brittany, remembering what she'd said.

"Surely you've heard about Shane Grant?" It was Darla who asked.

I shook my head.

Sure, I'd heard a few rumors. It was hard not to hear gossip about the rich and famous in a town like Aspen Valley, but I hadn't paid any real attention. Besides, it had never mattered. Until now.

Even now, I couldn't be sure it mattered.

"Just that he's pretty much known for not settling down," Brittany said. "He doesn't *date* women more than once or twice. Since his divorce, he hasn't really dated anyone in the sense of the word. He just has...well, hook-ups."

The part about not dating, he'd told me. But it seemed he may have glossed over the part about the hook-ups.

"And you thought that was a good thing?" I asked her.

"I did." She looked so genuine. "Jessie, you hadn't been out with a man in over a decade and I just thought that if you were out with Shane Grant, you'd probably have a whole lot of fun...but it wouldn't go anywhere. Just a one-night stand to shake the rust off. I mean, am I wrong, ladies? I know I'm not the only one who thought that night was going to be nothing more than a one-night stand."

Abby, Darla, and Sandy all shook their heads.

"You're not wrong," Darla said. "I was sure it would be a hot hook-up and that was it."

Abby nodded. "We were all surprised that you saw him again."

"And again," Sandy added.

My eyes went back to Brittany. "But you knew who he was and you didn't tell me."

"That's true."

"He played me." The pain bloomed fresh in my chest. "I fell for him, Brittany." Tears slipped from my eyes. "I fell so hard." I pulled in a shaky breath. "He made me feel things. And it wasn't just sex. It was so much more. He made me feel like he cared. That I was worthy of having a man care. He made me feel special. He gave me the confidence I needed to believe I could actually do something else. That I could finally follow my dreams and live my life for me. He opened my eyes to things that I never thought would be possible. And now—"

"Everything is still possible." Brittany had closed the distance between us. Sandy had slipped from the booth, making room for Brittany, who replaced her. She took my hands in hers and squeezed. "Your future is still yours, Jessie. I believe what I said about Shane. This felt different. He seemed to be genuinely upset that you were hurt. But regardless of him or what happens there, you don't need a man—any man—for that. Your future is yours and it is full of potential."

Tears blurred my vision, but I could see clearly that she believed what she was saying. She wasn't wrong. I didn't *need* a man.

"I know that's true," I said after a moment, tears still streaming down my cheeks. "But dammit, despite everything, I *want* that man."

Chapter Fifteen

"YOU'RE NOT GOING to punch me, are you?"

I considered it as I took the seat across from Trent at the club.

"No one is punching anyone," Phillip Conrad said.

I wasn't so sure of that yet, but it was probably a good thing that Phillip was there to act as a buffer.

"It's been awhile since we've all sat down for a drink, isn't it?" Phillip was trying for friendly and jovial.

I was feeling anything but.

I lifted my hand to the server. He knew my order and a few moments later, a whiskey appeared in front of me. I immediately took a sip and let the liquid warm me. But it wasn't enough. "It might be the last time." I pointed my look to Trent.

"Listen," he said. "It was business and you know it. I had no idea who she was to you."

"Who she *is*," I corrected him. Our relationship might be in tatters, but that didn't change how I felt about Jessie. If anything, it only made those feelings stronger.

"Right." Trent swallowed hard. "Of course."

I shook my head and looked away. Logically, I knew it

wasn't anything personal with Trent. He didn't know who Jessie was. I *knew* that. But logic or not, it still pissed me off. A lot.

"Abigail mentioned this deal to me a few days ago," Phillip said.

With everything going on, I'd almost forgotten that he was engaged to one of Jessie's best friends.

"She asked me to find a lawyer friend to look at things for Jessie."

I switched my glare to Phillip. "And you didn't?"

"Calm down, man." It was his turn to raise a hand. "You look like you might tear someone's head off."

It was entirely likely.

"Of course I did," Phillip said. "I contacted a buddy who specializes in property law right away. He promised to contact her immediately, but she didn't give him a chance. She signed before talking to him."

I returned my glare to Trent.

"I didn't pressure her," he said. "She texted me and told me she was ready to sign. Something must have changed her mind because I really wasn't convinced that she would. Not that easily."

The air escaped my lungs, and I slumped back in the chair. I'd spent the last few hours going over and over in my head what had happened and how it had gone wrong, and it all came down to one thing.

I lied.

It was my fault. If I had told her the truth about who I was, then maybe she would have trusted me with this information and I could have helped her. Maybe I would have been able to talk to Trent and to get her a reasonable deal.

Maybe. Maybe. Maybe.

I dropped my head in my hand, unable to look at my friends. It was my fault. I knew that now. I should have trusted that she was different than my ex. I should have trusted in what we had together.

Had.

No. What we *have.*

I wasn't willing to let go of it so easily. She was hurt right now. Of course she was. I couldn't blame her. But she wouldn't stay mad forever. Especially if I did everything in my power to fix this.

"What's the highest you would have gone?" I asked Trent when I lifted my head. "What's the highest offer you were willing to make? I know it was more. I know how this works."

He opened his mouth to argue with me but finally said, "A million. Maybe a million and a half."

My jaw dropped and Phillip let out a low whistle. "And what did she sign for?"

We all knew the answer and that it was woefully inadequate.

"I didn't know who she was to you, Shane. I mean, I still don't. But it's clear that she's important to you and—"

"It shouldn't matter who she is to me," I said with a shake of my head. "To rob someone of that much is—"

"Business," Trent interrupted. "Nothing more than business."

I shook my head. "Maybe so, but it's still shitty."

"It is shitty," Phillip agreed. "And ultimately, Aspen Valley is a small town. You don't want word to get out that you screwed over local business owners. It won't look good. Especially if you hope to do more business here in the future."

He was right, and I could see on his face that Trent knew it too. "Maybe it's different here than in the bigger cities."

I nodded.

"Okay," Trent said after a moment. "But the deals are done. It's not like I can change them now."

"Can't you?"

The idea came to me all at once. It was true that I'd hurt her so badly that Jessie might refuse to ever speak to me again, and I wouldn't blame her. But that wasn't going to change how I felt about her. I would do anything for Jessie. And it was time I proved it.

Sleep didn't come easily to me, but when it finally did, I felt like I could sleep forever. Maybe if I got lucky, I would. But who was I kidding? Luck was definitely not something I had.

Even so, after the girls met me at the diner and I cried myself out, they had taken me home and tucked me into bed like a child. It took forever to fall asleep and it felt like every time I did, I woke up with the fresh realization that my diner was gone because I'd fallen for a smooth-talking man who'd given me a little bit of attention.

So pathetic.

I'd fall asleep again after one of the ladies brought me hot tea and sat with me. All through the night, my girlfriends didn't leave. And when I woke up to the smell of pancakes coming from the kitchen the next morning after ten, I finally felt like myself again. Like maybe I'd slept away whatever version of myself had taken over my body for the last few weeks.

Jessie was back. And she was ready to make a plan and move forward.

"Good morning," Abby greeted me, spatula in hand. "Did you sleep finally?"

I nodded and gave Darla a grateful smile when she handed me a cup of coffee. "Thank you," I said to both of them. "For everything. I don't know what happened to me yesterday."

"I do," Darla said. "You hit a speed bump in life. A big one. It happens and it's okay to slow down."

She wasn't wrong. Even if the speed bump analogy felt

inadequate. I felt like I'd hit a brick wall that had been built in the middle of my life highway. "Did Sandy and Britt leave?" For the first time I noticed that the others were gone, which made sense. Sandy's mother-in-law was fantastic when it came to helping out with the girls, but they were still young and needed their mother more than a middle-aged woman having a life crisis. And Brittany...no doubt had to report to the office. And Shane.

It still hurt to think that she knew who he was the whole time and had kept his secret. But I believed her when she told me that she hadn't known about Trent Thomas or the acquisition offer. I still wasn't sure I believed her when she'd tried to tell me that Shane hadn't known either. How could that be true? Trent was his friend. He was in his office. He'd conveniently met me at the same time.

It added up.

And it still hurt like hell to think about.

That certainly hadn't faded overnight.

"They had things to take care of this morning," Abby said. "But they're going to meet us at the diner later."

"No." I shook my head. "I'm not going to the diner today."

Abby and Darla exchanged looks. "Why not? You still have—"

"I'm not going to open again," I said with certainty. It was a decision I'd come to at some point in the middle of the night. What was the point? It would only cost me money to stay open for a few more days. Never mind the emotional toll it would take to sit there, day after day, watching the business I'd built die a slow, painful death. Better to just rip off the bandage and move on. "It's over and the sooner I come to grips with that, the better."

I didn't miss the strange look that passed between them, but it was the smoke coming from behind Abby that pulled my attention. "Abby! You're—"

She turned at the same time and deftly flipped the charred pancakes from the pan and onto a plate. "Hungry?"

I couldn't help it; I burst out laughing. Darla joined in while Abby pretended to be offended.

"Maybe we should see if Stan will whip us up some breakfast?" I joked, but it didn't sound like a terrible idea.

"He might even be at Rosie's," Abby suggested. "I mean, did you tell them you weren't going to open today?"

Did I? I couldn't remember. The only thing I remembered was sending them both home the day before after they informed me that they were a couple and were ready to retire. I shook my head in disbelief, remembering that conversation now. *How could I not have seen it? Had I really been so buried in my life that I hadn't noticed the people around me? How long had I been like that?*

I knew the answer—far too long.

"I'll call." Darla pulled out her phone and started to connect the call. "I mean, no offense, Abby. But Stan's pancakes are a million times better than those."

"Hey," Abby protested. "You didn't even try them."

"We didn't have to," I said, unable to help myself from joining in the joking. It felt good to laugh after so much crying. "But I really do appreciate your effort," I added. "I appreciate you guys so much."

A huge smile spread across my friend's face. "I know you—"

"What?" Darla all but yelled into her phone, pulling my attention away from Abby. "That's....no way!"

"What?" I tried to get her attention. "What's happening? Is everything okay?"

"Okay," Darla said, ignoring me. "I'll tell her. We'll be right there." She hung up and finally turned to look at me. "We have to get down to Rosie's." Her face was blank of emotion. "There's something going on."

It felt like forever getting to Rosie's when in reality it couldn't have been more than twenty minutes. Darla was useless as far as giving me any information. She claimed she didn't know anything except that *something* was going on and we needed to get to the diner right away. Given the complete and total lack of information I'd been given, I didn't know what to expect when we pulled into the parking lot, but I didn't expect to find nowhere to park.

I couldn't remember the last time I'd seen so many cars in the lot. Probably because I'd *never* seen that many.

"What's going on here?" We got out of Abby's car—that we had to park in the empty lot of the dry cleaners—and made our way to Rosie's.

"It looks busy," Darla said. Her voice held an excited lilt.

"It's *never* busy."

"Sure looks busy to me," Abby agreed.

It *did* look busy, which was exactly why I was concerned. Rosie's was never busy. At least it hadn't been in months. Maybe even years, if I was honest. When the kids were little, it wasn't unusual to be packed during the dinner rush every day. The kids loved helping out. Clearing plates and carrying water jugs to the tables. And the customers loved it too. Who wouldn't love their cute little faces working hard to help Mom?

The memory hit me in the chest. Those days were long gone.

We hadn't needed more than one waitress—usually either Doris or me—for years. Let alone my two adorable helpers. "I better get in there." I picked up my pace, crossing the cracked asphalt. "Doris will be run off her—"

My words died on my lips when I opened the door and heard the jingle of the bells. I froze.

Just like the parking lot, my little diner was packed. A

banner had been strung over the counter that read, "We'll Miss You." There were giant bouquets of balloons in light pink and white all around the room. But it wasn't the decorations that I focused on. It was the people.

My eyes went directly to Sadie and Lucas. *What were they doing here?* I shook my head, and my hand flew to my mouth when I saw Stan and Doris next to them, their arms around each other. All through the room were the familiar faces of regular customers, friends and neighbors, including the owners of the dry cleaners that had closed, the gas station and the other businesses that had shared space with me for so long.

Tears sprang to my eyes as I took inventory of everyone and realized why they were all there. But I couldn't speak. Emotion flooded me and even with all of the tears I'd already shed, I was afraid that the moment I opened my mouth more would come.

Thankfully, I was saved from the shock by my friends. Abby and Darla guided me across the room to my children, whom I immediately pulled into a tight group hug. It hadn't been long but having my babies in my arms again filled a space inside me I didn't know was empty. I squeezed them tight and despite my efforts, tears slipped down my cheeks.

"God, it feels good to see you guys," I finally said when Lucas wiggled from my embrace. "But why are you here? We hadn't set a date yet for you to come home."

I turned around and once more scanned the room before looking back to them.

"Like we were going to miss this, Mom," Lucas said. "Why didn't you tell us what was going on?"

"Right?" Sadie said. "You should have told us."

They had a point but at the same time, I knew exactly why I hadn't told them. "It's not your responsibility," I said. "Your job is to focus on school and living your life. You shouldn't be worrying about this kind of thing."

"Mom." Sadie looked at me so seriously. It was looking at a mirror when I looked at her. "You *are* our life."

"Well," Lucas said with a grin. "Not our entire life."

Sadie nudged her twin brother, but they both laughed, and I couldn't help but smile.

"The point is," Abby came to stand next to me and Darla; Sandy and Brittany flanked my other side next to the kids, "you aren't alone, Jessie. And you don't have to do any of this on your own."

"We love you, Jessie." It was Darla.

I reached over and squeezed her hand.

"We're here for you."

"All of us," Sandy added.

"Don't forget us," Lucas added.

"I could never." I pulled my kids close again. Despite everything that had happened, when I had them there with me, everything seemed okay again. Except... "Oh, no." My hand flew to my mouth as I took a step back and looked at my children.

How was I supposed to tell them that I might not have enough money for them to continue their education? And that not only was the diner gone, but I might end up losing the house, too?

I swallowed hard. "I don't know how to tell you this, kids, but...your tuition is—"

"Isn't it amazing, Mom?"

"All four years," Lucas added, as if his sister's comment had made any sense.

"And," Sadie continued, "grad school options."

"And residence."

Their excitement was contagious. But mostly confusing. I wasn't sure I'd be able to pay for their second year of school, let alone the full four years. And I couldn't even think about graduate school and how much that would cost.

"Wait." I held my hand up. "Slow down. What are you talking about? Graduate school? We're going to have to——"

"The scholarships," Lucas said. "We got the email last night."

My mind spun, landing on random words they said. None of them made sense.

"Scholarships?"

Lucas nodded. "It was all in the——"

"Email?"

He sighed, so easily exasperated by his mother, and I couldn't blame him because I felt like I was in a fog, and nothing was making sense. *How long had I been asleep?*

"What scholarships?" I asked slowly.

Realization slid over my daughter's face. "You don't know."

I shook my head, and Sadie handed me her phone open to an email that laid it all out. A scholarship fund had been set up for my children from an anonymous donor. I blinked at the amount and looked up at my daughter, whose bright smile was stretched across her face. "It's so much." I barely muttered the words. "But…how…who…"

I knew the answer to that last one. There could only be one person who had the means to create a scholarship fund that would see my children through school, their living expenses, *and* the potential for master's programs.

Sadie took her phone from me before it could slip from my hands, which I could no longer feel.

"Pretty incredible, right, Mom?"

I nodded numbly at Lucas. "It really is. I don't know what to say."

"Do you know who did it?" Sadie asked. "I mean, it was so unexpected and——"

"I know."

I tried to look through the crowd, but my eyes landed on

Trent Thomas instead. He was walking toward me with an envelope.

What now?

"Let's give your mom a minute." Sandy ushered my kids away.

Brittany stood next to me, a fact I was grateful for because I could feel her spine stiffen as Trent drew nearer. She was a force to be reckoned with, and I was glad she was on my side.

"Ms. Bateman." He greeted me, and I didn't bother to remind him that we'd already been on a first-name basis. His eyes flicked over to Britt. "Have we met?"

There was a good chance they had met, of course, since Trent had been working in her offices, but she'd told me that she hadn't met him. And judging by the sharp look Brittany gave him, that was true. His eyes lingered on her for another moment before he looked back at me.

"There was a problem with the original contract," he said as he handed me the envelope. "I hope you find this one acceptable."

My heart sank. I simply could not do this again. I yanked my hand back from the envelope. "We already signed, Mr. Thomas. It's done."

"I think you'll find this contract more...complete." He waved the envelope, but I still wouldn't take it. "Ms. Bateman, I—"

Brittany snatched it from him.

I gave her a little nod, and she opened it. I kept my gaze down on the familiar black and white vinyl floor tiles, tracing the lines with my eyes until I felt Britt's hand on my shoulder.

"Jessie? You should look at this."

When I lifted my head, she nodded reassuringly and handed me the papers. My hands shook as I skimmed the words written there. It was exactly the same as the contract I'd already signed. I didn't understand. Until I got to the dollar amount.

I took a stumbling step backward, but Abby was still on the other side of me and caught me with an arm around my shoulders.

I read the amount again. And again, until the number blurred in my vision.

"I don't understand." I finally lifted my head to look at Trent Thomas, who waited patiently. "But I already——"

"That wasn't an acceptable offer." He cut me off. "I do hope you find that this one is adequate."

Adequate? It was more than ten times the original offer.

My mouth opened and closed. I swallowed hard and nodded.

"Good." Trent smiled. He handed me a pen, and I signed my name quickly. He folded the paper and tucked it into his suit jacket. "Jessie, I want you to know how sorry I am for not making this offer in the first place." His smile faded and his eyes filled with sincerity. "I want you to know that your neighbors," he waved his hand a little, "the other businesses…they also got signing bonuses that are more appropriate to what they've given up."

Signing bonuses? More money?

I shook my head, unclear on what he'd said.

"Sometimes I get wrapped up in the business side of what I do, and I forget that there are real people's lives on the line," he continued. "This time I needed a little reminder," he said. "I am truly sorry."

I believed him. "Thank you, Mr. Thomas."

"Trent."

"Trent." I even managed a small smile as I shook his hand. Before he turned to walk away, I had to know for sure. "Who reminded you?"

His eyes sparkled, and I watched as he looked to Brittany

quickly. But it wasn't her. I already knew the answer. Just like I already knew that Dax—or Shane as I should probably get used to calling him—was standing across the room. I could feel his eyes on me. I'd felt him the moment I walked into the diner.

Trent stepped to the side and there he was.

He wore his familiar dark jeans, but instead of the leather vest that I realized belatedly was likely still at my house, he wore a crisp black button-down shirt and a suit jacket. He looked incredible. My heart squeezed tight in my chest, making it hard to breathe.

I froze when he started to walk toward me. My friends—who just a moment before had told me they were there for me—had somehow miraculously melted away. I was on my own.

My body instinctively leaned forward as he approached. More than anything, I wanted to be pressed up against his chest, his strong arms wrapped around me and holding me close.

At the same time, I wanted to hit him. Scream at him. And tell him to leave me alone forever.

"Hi." His voice was low, but the moment I heard it, so much of the anger I was holding melted away.

"Hi."

"If you want me to, I'll leave."

I was certain all eyes were on us, but music had started playing and vaguely I recognized that conversations were happening all around me. It was a party. But I couldn't look away from Shane. From the man who'd captured my heart and subsequently shattered it, all in only a few weeks.

"Jessie?"

"You lied to me."

He flinched, as if my words caused him physical pain.

"I did."

"You hurt me."

Again, his eyes squeezed closed against my words. Shane

nodded. "It's the last thing in the world I ever wanted to do," he said when he opened his eyes. "I know you have no reason to believe me, Jessie. But I swear to you that everything that happened between us was real. Everything. It had nothing to do with Brittany or Trent or any acquisition or…anything. It was all us. Me and you. Never in my entire life have I felt this way about a woman. And I know it's all happened so fast and the timing…fuck. The timing sucks."

Understatement.

"But I can't change that," he continued. "And I wouldn't change a thing because if I did, it would mean that we would never have met and my life wouldn't have been changed forever. Because whether you tell me to leave and never come back, or not, my entire life has been changed, Jessie. After only a few weeks with you, I know something I never knew before."

I looked up, curious.

"I know now what it's supposed to feel like," he said and I almost melted. "I know that all of these years when I was looking for an escape, I should have been searching for a connection. But even if I'd been looking for it back then, it wouldn't have mattered. Because I wouldn't have met you. And the connection I have with you, Jessie…well, it's beyond anything I could have ever imagined. You can ask me to leave and I will. But I hope like hell you don't."

Despite my hurt, I could see the truth in his eyes.

"You did this?" I used my head to gesture to the party going on all around us.

"I had a lot of help," he said. "But I need you to know, Jessie. I would do anything for you." He shook his head. "I *will* do anything for you," he corrected.

That was almost my undoing. Tears burned in the corners of my eyes. I squeezed my eyes shut against the warring feelings battling within me. I wanted to believe him. I wanted to believe who he was and how he felt. I wanted more than anything to believe it was all true.

"Dance with me."

I opened my eyes to see his hand waiting for mine.

"Please," he added. "You never have to see me again, Jessie. I'll walk away and never bother you again if that's what you want."

It's not! I wanted to scream it, but I couldn't.

"But first," he continued. "I need you to hear me out. Please. Dance with me."

My body moved forward on its own. The moment my hand slid into his, heat traveled through me, warming the chill I couldn't seem to shake for the last twenty-four hours. But when he pulled me into his arms, something inside me clicked into place.

"I should have told you who I was from the beginning."

Our bodies moved together with the rhythm of a song playing in the background.

"Yes," I said simply. "You should have."

"I didn't expect it to be more than one night."

"Neither did I."

"I couldn't stay away from you," Shane said. "Not then, not now." His feet stopped moving. With one finger, he tilted my chin up so I stared straight into his silver eyes. "Dax is my middle name," he said seriously. "My full name is Shane Dax Grant. I'm the only child of Bonnie and Maurice Grant, who are happily retired and spend their days playing golf in Arizona. I am the CEO and founder of MultiTech Software, which means I am quite well off."

I felt like that was an understatement, but I didn't say so.

"I was married once before to a woman who used me for my money, broke my heart, and left me jaded," he continued. "Trent Thomas is an old college friend of mine." His voice lowered and he looked me directly in the eyes. "He is in town and using my offices temporarily. I had no idea it was your diner he was acquiring. Not until I saw you in my offices. I didn't know."

I took a deep breath. "I believe you."

Relief washed over his handsome face. "You do?"

I breathed out slowly and nodded. "I do," I said with one hundred percent conviction.

"Is that everything?" I needed to know. "Is there anything else you're keeping from me, Shane?"

His eyes closed, he nodded once, and my heart sank. I couldn't do this. I couldn't let myself be hurt again. It was too much. I tried to pull out of his arms, but he held me tight.

"There is one more thing I need to tell you, Jessie."

I squeezed my eyes and shook my head. I didn't want to hear it.

"And I need you to hear it clearly."

Still, I wouldn't open my eyes.

He took a breath and exhaled slowly. "I'm in love with you, Jessie. I said it once before, but I should have made sure you heard me. I need you to know it."

My eyes flew open. I took a staggering step back, but Shane pulled me tight, so he was pressed up against me.

"I love you, Jessie Bateman." His eyes sparkled, and his lips curled into a handsome smile. "I know it's fast and I know that we—"

"I love you, too."

His lips crushed mine in a kiss before I even realized what I'd said. But I wouldn't have changed it. I did love him. Completely. Yes, he'd lied. But if I could look past my own hurt for a minute, I could understand why. And it didn't matter because, fundamentally, I *knew* him. And he knew me. And that was all that mattered.

His feet started to move again to the rhythm of the music, and my body followed, as if we were the only two people in the room. I tucked my head against his chest and let myself feel everything.

My diner was sold. For a ridiculous amount of money, which meant I had the freedom to explore what I wanted to do next without any pressure.

The kids' education was taken care of. They wouldn't have to worry and could focus on their studies. I knew Shane was responsible; I'd thank him later.

But most importantly, this incredible man, who made me feel things I'd never felt and who in such a short time had opened my life up to things I'd never thought possible, *loved* me.

And I loved him.

"Everything is changing," I said aloud.

"Does that frighten you?"

"A little," I answered honestly.

"I understand." Shane nodded and pulled me in closer. "But remember our rules?"

"Hold on," I said, feeling his strong back under my fingers. "And—"

"Let go." Shane finished for me.

His lips once more pressed to mine, and that's exactly what I did. Because now I knew how good letting go could feel.

Epilogue

TWO MONTHS LATER...

I didn't get nervous. Ever.

But having Jessie's kids stay with us for the weekend definitely made me nervous. Not that I had a reason to be—at least not one that Jessie knew about. After all, since that day in the diner when Jessie and I finally put everything behind us and made the decision to follow our *rules*, we'd spent a lot of times as a family.

Family.

It was still a word I was getting used to. In all the best ways.

As an only child, I had no idea what it was like to have a full house. And I'd never wanted children of my own. Not really. Sure, there'd been a moment where I thought Courtney and I might...but that was so short-lived, any ideas I'd had about being a father had died along with that relationship.

Until now.

Sadie and Lucas were great kids. Not that they could be anything else considering they were Jessie's, and she'd raised them to be as amazing as she was. Still. I was nervous about what they would think when I—

"You really need to stop pacing." Jessie laughed as I made my third lap around our kitchen.

Our kitchen. It felt so good to say that. We'd only been together for two months, but I'd known without a doubt that Jessie was my forever from almost the first moment I met her, so two months felt like a long time. Still, it had taken almost that long for me to convince Jessie to move in with me.

Her little house was comfortable, but she said herself it wasn't really *home*. Still, she was hesitant. Not that I could blame her after our less than smooth start. Still. I wanted her in my bed—our bed—every night and drinking coffee in *our* kitchen. And life was short. We'd spent the first half of our lives without each other; I didn't want to waste one more minute without her. The minute she agreed to move in with me, we started shopping for the house that we could make a home together.

And we'd found it.

It was five minutes out of town. Far enough to be private, with our very own forest in the backyard in the shadow of the mountains, but close enough to get to the office quickly and out with our friends. Jessie, who was new to the amount of money we now had—I told her more than once that what was mine was hers, and I meant it—wanted to buy a small house with only a few bedrooms in a modest neighborhood. I had never had a house before, preferring penthouse apartments.

We settled on an eight-bedroom, brick ranch-style house. It was fully fenced with professionally cared for gardens, a pool, and a guesthouse that Jessie had turned into her studio, having recently rediscovered her love for painting. I loved watching how quickly her passion had come back to her now that she had time to enjoy it.

I loved watching how happy she was after a day in her

studio. Making love to her on the kitchen island, still covered in paint from her efforts. Ever since selling the diner, she'd blossomed, and watching it filled me with love I didn't even know I was capable of.

"You know the kids love you." Jessie came up behind me, wrapped her arms around my waist, and slid her hands to my belt buckle.

Instantly, I sprang to life. The woman had an immediate effect on me.

And she knew it.

Her fingers worked at my belt and slid into my jeans, where they wrapped around my length, already hard for her. I groaned. "They're going to be here any minute."

She squeezed. "They're not here yet."

It was a good point. I spun her around and pushed her against the wall, crushing my mouth to hers.

A *very* good point.

She wore a skirt. Something she'd been doing more and more because I could never get enough of her bare legs. Also, the skirts had the added benefit of me being able to slide my hands up them easily.

"Have I told you today how much I love you?"

"Only a half dozen times," she said as I pulled her panties aside.

I lifted her easily, and she wrapped her legs around my back. "Oh, I'm behind schedule."

Her mouth formed the sexiest little circle as I entered her with a thrust. She was wet and ready for me. Always. The way I always, inexplicably, was ready for her.

We moved together quickly. It was true that we would have guests any moment. A fact we were both very aware of.

We came quickly. Jessie with a satisfied moan, I with a shuddering groan. Only moments later, the doorbell rang, followed by Sadie calling out her greeting.

"How was that for timing?" Jessie straightened her clothes and kissed me quickly on the cheek.

I pulled her back into me for another kiss before releasing her to greet her children. "I love you, Jessie."

"I know it." Her smile was everything. "And I love you."

As cute as it was that Shane was nervous about the kids coming to visit, I truly didn't see anything for him to be concerned about. Both Sadie and Lucas had fallen in love with him almost as quickly as I had.

They deserved a strong father figure in their life, and even though I'd never asked him, Shane never hesitated to jump in. Not even once.

I know how badly he wanted the weekend to go well and how much he wanted the kids to like our new home. Obviously, they did. How could they not?

We'd had their rooms professionally decorated in colors of their choosing. The game room in the basement had a pool table, pinball games, darts, and various other video game consoles. Never mind the outdoor heated pool they were going to enjoy this summer when they came back for their break between semesters.

It was a beautiful house. And it was *ours*.

True, Shane bought it. He'd insisted. But he'd also insisted that both our names were on the title. He knew I didn't love him for his money. I loved him for who he was. And sometimes I still called him Dax when I was feeling particularly naughty.

I could hardly believe it was my life sometimes. How had I gotten so lucky to find a man who loved every single inch of me, treated me like a goddess, loved and cared for my kids, *and* was a super-wealthy billionaire?

"I want to make a toast," Shane said now.

We'd just finished our first dinner all together in the house. The kids were each going out to visit with their friends because they were only in town for the weekend, and I had my weekly catch-up with the girls later. This time at Sandy's house, where we'd been meeting since Rosie's was officially closed. Brittany had made a comment via text earlier about needing to vent. I had a sneaking suspicion it had something to do with Trent Thomas, who even after the whole acquisition debacle, I'd come to know and love as one of Shane's best friends. He was still working out of Shane's offices, and I hadn't missed the way he'd looked at Britt back at the diner. Or, more importantly, the way she'd pretended not to notice.

Shane waited while we all raised our glasses. "To Sadie and Lucas," Shane said. "Thank you for welcoming me into your lives so freely and sharing your mother with me."

Sadie clasped a hand to her chest and tears sprang to my eyes at her reaction.

"It's you we should be thanking, Shane," Lucas said. Sadie nodded when he looked at his sister, but he continued. "We've never seen Mom look so happy and…"

"She deserves it," Sadie finished. "You really do, Mom."

There was no help for it. The tears slipped down my cheek. "That means a lot."

Shane cleared his throat and we all looked back to him. He'd put his glass down and now held a box in his hand.

I tilted my head and stared at him. We'd talked about marriage. But dismissed it. He'd had a horrible first experience and my own marriage hadn't been anything to get excited about. *What was he—*

"Before you say no," Shane said quickly. "This doesn't have to be anything."

He moved from his chair to one knee in front of me. Sadie made a squeaking sound, but I couldn't look away from Shane.

"But I want you to know," he said, "that this represents

everything. Jessie, you own me. You have my heart, completely and forever. Whether we make it legal by signing papers or not, that doesn't and will never change how I feel about you, and I want the whole world to know my level of commitment for you today and always."

He opened the box then, and the ring inside took my breath away. It was a brilliantly blue sapphire, with two diamonds set on either side.

"Shane. It's beautiful."

"The sapphire represents you," he said. "And the diamonds are for the kids."

My hand flew to my mouth, and I swallowed a sob. It was the single sweetest thing anyone had ever given me.

"So?" Shane took the ring from the box and held it out to me. "Will you be forever mine?"

"Of course. I already am." He slipped the ring on my finger and stood, pulling me up with him.

We sealed it with a kiss, and then the kids were up and out of their seats. We were all hugging and crying, and it was absolutely perfect.

Forever mine. Shane's words echoed in my head as I watched him with Sadie and Lucas. My family.

Finally.

Finally, *mine.*

***

I hope you enjoyed Jessie and Shane's journey to love. As a special treat...click HERE for an alternate scene to Jessie and Shane's date night at the sushi resturant.
And next...
It's Brittany's turn next as she decides to *go for it*.

But will Trent play along and be a willing participant?
And what happens when their little arrangment
threatens to turn into more?
Find out next in Finally Fell

And if you want even more romance...click <u>HERE</u> for
an exclusive FREE novella that isn't available
anywhere else!

Finally Fell

It's Brittany's turn to FINALLY find her Happily Ever After
Please enjoy this unedited excerpt in Finally Fell

The ladies' room was a welcome reprieve. The moment I stepped through the doors and they closed behind me, dulling the din of the constant conversation and background music, both of which seemed to be louder than usual, I felt like I could breathe again.

Mercifully, the restroom seemed to be empty. The only thing worse than making small talk with a never-ending flow of colleagues and clients was doing it in the washroom. Despite myself, I chuckled at the thought of discussing the latest financials with the CEO of Multitech, the company I was currently the Chief Financial Officer of, while we touched up our makeup. Especially since the CEO was Shane Grant, a rather large, bearded man.

In fact, most of my colleagues were men. Escaping to the ladies' room alone was one of the very few perks of being one of the only women in a high-powered executive role. I'd worked hard to be in the position I was in. A few minutes of respite from these events, shouldn't be too much of an ask.

Shouldn't be.

I inhaled deeply and tried to shake the melancholy that was hanging over me. I usually loved these events. I'd dedicated my life to my career and not one time had it been a hardship. While my best friends were getting married, I was working late into the night, choosing the hardest accounts to prove myself. When they were having babies and going to Mommy and Me classes, I was wining and dining clients, fending off inappropriate advances and proving myself a loyal and indispensable asset to the business by working sixty-hour workweeks. When they were buying houses and hosting dinner parties, I was living off take-out while I worked by the dim glow of my computer screen well past midnight.

And I loved it.

Never once had I felt like I'd missed out.

Not one time did I wish I'd chosen a different path in life.

I thrived on the challenge of my career. Working the numbers, finding opportunities to grow a company through the bottom line. It was exhilarating.

And these black tie nights were all part of it.

I used to live for this shit. Schmoozing potential clients, or merger opportunities was my jam. And I was good at it. Stuffy corporate types, never saw me coming. They saw a tall, good-looking blond with red lipstick, and instantly their guard fell. Those were the easy ones. The ones who thought with their dick first. The ones who didn't even consider that a pretty girl could possibly have the brains to know a thing about money, let alone how it could be used to the ultimate advantage.

And then there were men like Shane Grant, my boss. He was one of the good ones. He not only recognized how smart I was, but how advantageous I could be for him in his tech company. The thing that people didn't know about tech companies, was that innovation was only a small part of the job. The bigger job was buying up the constant flow of start-ups that popped up and threatened your business.

And that's where I came in.

Not only could I boil down the numbers into a bottom line that would benefit everyone, nobody expected it from me. It only took me a few minutes of conversation with a potential acquisition target to know what I needed to know. It was amazing what men would say after a few minutes of flirting with a pretty woman. More often than not, before the first drink was done I knew about their cash flow—usually their lack of it—their bottom line and exactly how much—or how little—it would take to buy them up.

I was damn good at my job.

But more and more lately it was starting to feel empty. The heady rush that used to fuel me was slowly being replaced with disappointment. It's not that it wasn't challenging anymore. It was. That was the thing about working with numbers and people. There was always a challenge to sink my teeth into.

Still…I couldn't help feeling that there was more to life. It was troubling that I'd been feeling that way more often lately. Especially since I didn't know what *more* meant.

With a sigh, I examined my reflection. I'd been gone long enough. I would need to get back out there before my presence was missed. Despite the fact that my bright red lipstick was still perfectly applied, I pulled the tube from my clutch and carefully reapplied a coat. My long blond hair had been pulled up into a tight twist at the back of my head leaving my neck bare. The dress I'd chosen was black and elegant. Cut deep enough in the front to be sexy, but not slutty. Just enough to catch the eye. It was long-sleeved, but off the shoulder with a low back. It was more skin than I usually exposed at a work function, but I didn't care. The dress looked amazing. And I felt fabulous in it.

There was a mid-thigh slit in the long skirt that offered glimpses of my lean legs that I knew looked impressive with the red stilettos I'd chosen to match my signature lipstick.

I capped the lipstick and returned it to my purse as the door of the restroom opened with a wave of noise. A giggling redhead who'd clearly had one too many drinks for a work function all but fell into the room before the door shut behind her.

"Oh, I didn't—hi," the girl said as she noticed me for the first time. She straightened up and made her way to the sink. "I didn't realize there was anyone in here."

I shrugged a little, not remotely interested in starting a conversation. If I was going to be subjected to small talk, I wasn't going to be doing it in the bathroom with someone's drunk date.

I turned to leave.

"Sorry," the girl said, stopping me. "Would you mind…"

I turned to see her shimming her body awkwardly as she reached up behind her back.

"This zipper…it's…"

"Sure." I put my clutch on the counter and rescued the girl from her skin-tight dress by working the zipper down her back far enough that she could manage the rest. "There you go."

"You're a lifesaver. Thank you." She shuffled to a stall as she wiggled the fabric up around her hips. "I don't know why they make these dresses so impossible," she spoke through the closed door. "I mean, I can hardly sit down, let alone pull it up enough to pee." A giggle filled the air as I moved to leave. "Oh!" She shouted out. "Can you please wait a minute?" *Could she read minds?* I froze and stared at the closed door. "I won't be able to get back into my dress," she continued. "Please."

It's not like I could say no. "Okay."

"You are a saint." She laughed again and I heard a flush before she emerged, looking visibly relieved. "Thank you so much." She washed her hands while I waited. "My name is Trista, by the way. This is my first time at one of these," she continued without waiting for a response. "It's so fun, don't you think?"

I didn't. Fun was not a word I'd ever use to describe these functions. Not even when I was Trista's age. "You look like you've been to one or two before," she continued. "I mean, I'm probably the youngest one here. Don't you think?"

Was she saying I was old?

I swallowed hard and waited for her to turn around so I could zip her up and get out of there. My little break was quickly turning into a reminder that the only thing I hated more than small talk, was making it with the bimbo dates that some of the men insisted on bringing to these functions. As if dating a girl who was barely over the legal drinking age was going to make them feel any younger. Hell, maybe it did. But it sure didn't make them look anything but desperate and more than a little ridiculous.

"Nice to meet you, Trista." I gave her a bright smile. "And yes, you are definitely one of the younger women here, but don't let that intimidate you. I was once—"

"Oh, I'm not." I watched as she reached into her dress and lifted first one of her huge breasts into place in her dress and then the other, before turning to present her back and the zipper to me. "I mean I am the prettiest girl in the room. No offence." I tugged her zipper up sharply making her gasp.

"None taken."

I was quickly losing my patience with this girl.

"But you have to admit," Trista said as she spun to face the mirror and fluff her hair. "These places are perfect for finding a rich guy, right? I mean all it takes is a quick blow job in the car on the way home and they're in love, am I right?" She winked. "You look like you know exactly what I mean."

I did?

"Oh, definitely." I nodded. "If you'll excuse me, Trista. I should get back."

"Of course." She pursed her lips together seriously. "You can't keep them waiting. These guys need so much attention."

It was an effort not to roll my eyes as I left her primping her ridiculously young, firm body and rejoined the party. The thing was, Trista wasn't wrong. The majority of the men at these events were either on their second, third or fourth wife, each younger than the last, or they were there with a girl like Trista.

It was a gross overgeneralization of course, and there were exceptions. But I couldn't help but think that those exceptions were getting harder and harder to find. Not that I was looking.

I wasn't.

The only man I needed in my life was one to scratch the occasional itch before getting out of my bed and back to his own apartment before the sun came up. Period.

"Brittany! Just the woman I was looking for."

I turned my smile perfectly in place to greet my boss, Shane Grant who also happened to be my best friend Jessie's new boyfriend. It was a long story, but they were perfect for each other. Making Shane Grant one of those very rare exceptions I was just thinking about.

"Shane." I leaned in as he greeted me with a kiss on the cheek. "Jessie." I pulled my friend in for a hug. I knew she'd feel a little out of place at the club, but I loved that she was here. "You look amazing."

She really did. Ever since she'd sold her diner and fallen completely into her new relationship with Shane, she was like a totally different woman. She deserved it, too.

"Thank you." Jessie twirled a little in her dress. "But seriously, Britt. You look amazing."

Shane put his arm around Jessie's waist and pulled her close. "I'm a little partial," he said as he kissed her on the cheek. "But Jessie really does look incredible." He flashed a smile at me. "Brittany, you look exceptional as always."

I laughed. "Thanks, Shane. It's been a good night. I had an interesting conversation with Chad Duvall. I think he'll be open to a meeting next week." I spent the next few minutes filling him in on my conversations so far before his attention was distracted.

"Sorry, Brittany," he said as he waved at someone behind me. "But I have to change the subject quickly." He looked to Jessie again. "I know a lot went down between you," he said to her. "And I know you've had the chance to clear the air, but it's important to me that you two get to know each other as friends. And Brittany, even though he's been sharing our office space, I don't think you've properly met him either."

I didn't have to turn around to see who Shane was talking about. My spine stiffened, and at the same time, my stomach flipped. I'd only actually met him once when he rectified his terrible behaviour in acquiring Jessie's diner. We'd hardly even spoken to each other at that meeting, still, I'd had a very hard time getting his green eyes out of my mind. The way he'd looked at me. No man had ever looked at me that way before and I couldn't quite put my finger on why it was different. Only that it was. And it made me feel things. A lot of things. Things that had followed me into my dreams. It was true, he was sharing office space with us at MultiTech. It was also true that I'd done my best to avoid him and his unnerving gaze.

But I couldn't ignore him forever. He *was* a good friend of my Shane's. Besides, I didn't even know him. And it was probably just a one-time, chance thing that I'd misread.

I put my well-practiced smile in place and slowly turned around as Shane greeted him.

"Trent! Good to see you, man."

But it wasn't a one-time thing. The second I turned around, my eyes locked on Trent Thomas's green gaze and it happened again. The look. Like he could *see* me. Like he *knew* me. Like he *wanted* me. All of me.

My breath hitched in my throat in a way that made it hard to breathe but I didn't look away. Neither did he. It wasn't until Shane said, "And who is your beautiful date tonight?" That I finally tore my gaze away from Trent's, to see the woman I hadn't noticed until then.

Trista.

#

Brittany Donahue.

Damn.

Somehow every time I saw the woman she looked sexier than the last. Her glacier blue eyes pierced me, challenging me. But I held her gaze unwavering until my date tugged on my arm, at the exact same moment Brittany looked away.

"Hi," the girl next to me whose name I'd momentarily forgotten, cooed. "I'm Trista."

Trista. Right.

She thrust her hand out along with her massive tits and tossed her hair over her shoulder with a giggle as Shane politely took her hand in greeting. She was so obvious it was embarrassing. Mostly for her, but I couldn't help but cringe.

My gaze moved back to Brittany who didn't bother to hide her look of disgust at Trista's behaviour. As if she sensed me, she looked up and raised an eyebrow in question as if to say, "*Really?*"

In response, I pressed my lips together and shrugged a little before introducing my date to Jessie. "Shane's fiancé." I made a point to emphasize the word because even though Trista was there with me, she was definitely the type to look for a bigger and better opportunity.

I knew the type. Hell, I knew it well. I'd only exclusively dated Trista's for years.

Young, giggly, big tits that looked good in a tight dress, and even better in my hands.

Dating Trista's was easy.

She got what she wanted, treated to expensive dinners, drinks and occasional gifts with the opportunity to meet her next sugar daddy and I got what I wanted—a plus one at these boring events followed by a hot fuck before going home alone, just the way I liked it.

And it was how I liked it.

Trista, messaged received, had resumed her rubbing up on my side. Her tits pressed into me and one hand slid down over my ass.

I cleared my throat and took a small hopefully subtle step to the side.

Brittany swallowed a chuckle.

Not so subtle then.

I ignored her and focused on Shane and Jessie. "How are the two of you?" I looked directly at Jessie who had every reason to hate me after I'd tried to acquire her diner, Rosie's for a pittance a few months earlier. To be fair, it was only business and I would have done the exact same thing no matter who it was. Still, when I learned that she was involved with Shane and —more importantly—realized for the first time how *just doing business* could impact real people and real lives, I took a different approach to the acquisitions division of my business. A much more humane approach. So far, not only had it worked, it made me feel like a better person to make fair deals with people instead of trying to get the lowest possible price for my bottom line. It felt good and I had Jessie to thank for that. Something I'd done repeatedly ever since making amends with her.

Still, her friend Brittany clearly hadn't gotten the memo.

Ice Queen would be a generous description of the woman who stood silently glaring at me next to Jessie, almost as if she were on guard, as the three of us made small talk for a few minutes.

"I'm so sorry," Shane said, changing the subject abruptly. "I wanted to make sure the two of you had been properly introduced." He gestured for Brittany to step forward. She did so, but the mask of indifference on her gorgeous face remained firmly in place.

"We've met," I said. Still, I held my hand out wanting to touch her. "But it never hurts to have a proper introduction after everything that's transpired." I gave her my most charming smile as I carefully shook Trista off my left side. "It is absolutely my pleasure to officially meet you, Brittany. My good friend Shane here speaks very highly of you."

For a moment, I was certain she was going to snub me altogether. My hand dangled in the space between us, but I was a patient man. I focused my eyes on her, but she didn't quite meet my gaze. I was almost ready to admit defeat when her red lips very deliberately moved into what had to be a carefully practiced smile. "Trent." Her voice oozed with social graces. Oh yes, she knew exactly what she was doing. But when her manicured hand finally slipped into mine, her carefully constructed persona faltered.

I saw it, even if no one else noticed when her chest hitched with a sharp intake of breath as my fingers held hers in a soft, but firm grip.

Heat flashed between us, and even I had a hard time not reacting to what should have been an innocent touch.

"It's..." she worked hard to recover without incident. "It's very nice to finally meet you in better circumstances." She held her smile on her face as finally, her eyes met mine. Again, her pupils dilated making her pale blue eyes darken. *With lust?*

Damn. I couldn't know with certainty that's what she was feeling. But fuck, it was most definitely what I was feeling.

One. Simple. Touch.

As quick as it was there, it was gone. She'd withdrawn her hand, her gaze once more fixed just over my shoulder.

"Aren't you both in the same office?" Jessie asked, oblivious as was everyone else as to what had just transpired between us. "How is it you've never run into each other?"

It was an excellent question. One I was pretty sure I already knew the answer to.

"If I didn't know better," I said with just enough mischief in my voice to keep it light. "I'd think that Brittany's been avoiding me."

I saw the flinch. I was right. She *had* been avoiding me. But why?

"Why would I be avoiding you?" Her voice didn't reveal anything. "After all, I don't even know you."

Jessie looked between her friend and back to me. Out of the corner of my eye, I saw her roll her eyes. So, I wasn't the only one who recognized that something was up with Brittany.

But if Jessie thought her friend was acting strange, there must be some kind of secret friendship pact, because she didn't say anything, but swiftly changed the subject to ask about the development that was going in where her diner had once stood.

Distracted, I did my best not to be rude to her especially since we were tentatively building a friendship after our rocky start and answered all of her questions as Shane and Brittany fell into a separate conversation beside us. Distractedly, I realized Trista had found her way to the bar—again—and the bartender who didn't try to hide the fact that he was ogling her breasts as he poured her stronger than necessary drinks

I shook my head slightly. I'd peel her away from the bar later, after all, even annoying and vapid, she was still my date. And her tits *were* magnificent.

"So what do you think, Trent?"

I cleared my head and refocused on the conversation which

had clearly shifted again. Shane was watching me and waiting for an answer. "What do you think?"

"Sounds good."

"It does?" Shane raised his eyes.

Shit. It was the wrong answer apparently. But, I was invested now. "Why not?" I said with confidence.

"Looks like you're outvoted, Shane," Jessie said next to me.

"You're supposed to be on my side, man," Shane said with a groan, but despite the fact that he'd obviously conceded to whatever it was his girlfriend wanted, he didn't look upset. But I was still confused.

"Do I get a vote?" Brittany asked.

"No way," Jessie jumped in. "You're my friend so obviously you agree with me."

"Sure," Brittany said with an emphasized smile. "A dinner party sounds like fun, Jessie. I can't wait."

So that's what I'd agreed to. It could be worse. I didn't mind a dinner party among friends. It was definitely better than these stuffy affairs, and even they weren't all bad. There were worse things than being surrounded by gorgeous women. And that was definitely one of the perks of these things. My eyes settled on Brittany who looked damned good in her black off-the-shoulder dress. It was fitted and clung to her in all the right ways. Her body was long and lean, her breasts smaller than what usually caught my eye, but still beautiful. In fact, everything about Brittany was stunning. Elegant in a way that demanded attention and respect.

"Not a dinner party," Jessie corrected. "A *housewarming* party." She laughed. "Super casual. Just a few friends."

"Tell me when," I said with a smile as Trista reappeared at my side and threaded her arm through mine. "I'll be there."

I heard Shane mutter *traitor*, but he chuckled as he said it. It was no secret that he'd do anything for Jessie. My friend who'd once been burned so badly by a woman that he'd sworn off any relationship longer than one night, was completely head over heels and one hundred percent devoted to the single mom.

And if it could happen to Shane...

My eyes drifted down to Trista who was looking up at me with hooded lids full of promise. Or too much alcohol. Either way, it was definitely time to take her home. But it wasn't my date who held my attention as I quickly said our goodbyes.

"It was nice to properly meet you, Trent." Brittany's voice gave nothing away, but I was certain I heard the slightest trace of sarcasm there. Her eyes sparkled as she winked in my direction.

I took her hand again, this time squeezing it just a little as the heat flowed between us. "I hope to see you soon, Brittany." I looked straight into her eyes so I didn't miss the flash in them. "Now that I know you're not avoiding me."

Her cheeks pinked. Not enough for anyone else to notice, except me as she withdrew her hand, clearly flustered.

I turned to leave, Trista still glued to my left side.

"Enjoy the rest of your night."

Brittany's voice reached me and just like that, I knew there was only one way I'd be enjoying the rest of my night. And unfortunately, that wasn't likely to happen.

Read the rest of Finally Fell NOW!

About the Author

Elena Aitken is a USA Today Bestselling Author of more than forty romance and women's fiction novels. The mother of 'grown up' twins, Elena now lives with her very own mountain man in the heart of the very mountains she writes about. She can often be found with her toes in the lake and a glass of wine in her hand, dreaming up her next book and working on her own happily ever after.

To learn more about Elena:
www.elenaaitken.com
elena@elenaaitken.com